Illuminated Darkness

OTS #5

Audrey Brice

Darkerwood Publishing Group

U.S.A.

2019

Darkerwood Publishing Group, Arvada, CO

ISBN: 978-1-938839-10-8

Thank you to Will and Shaelyn for your willingness to line edit and go over this story, and to offer feedback.

http://www.the-quadrant.com

Sign up for the Audrey Brice Newsletter to receive **free fiction** and updates on new releases!

Books in the OTS Series: Outer Darkness (1), Into Darkness (2), Rising Darkness (3), Ascending Darkness (4), Illuminated Darkness (5) and Within Darkness (a collection of OTS novellas)

For Lucifuge, whose inspiration brings illumination.

CHAPTER 1

Daemonic possession stories never account for the fact that Daemons can be smart asses. You're probably wondering how I know this. Let's just say that ever since I upset Monica Niel's Blood of Saturn operation, the one she ran out of the now-defunct shop, The Cloven Hoof, Lucifuge started hanging out with me on a regular basis. Who would have known a single invocation for strength would have served as an invitation for the Daemon to stick around long after the need for his power was over? Lesson learned.

It's not that I regretted my choice to invoke Lucifuge that ill-fated night, but let's just say that the Daemon wasn't forthcoming about why he'd chosen me as his vessel. Not at first.

My name is Elizabeth Tanner, and I'm a magician. The story I'm about to tell you is true.

***

The Daemon had started popping in on me at regular intervals, watching everything I was doing and offering advice where appropriate, but never quite telling me why he was hanging around. The only thing he mentioned was that he was my *protectorate*. On this particular day, all of that changed.

I like the Goetia programming, Lucifuge told me.

"You would," I murmured to the Daemon. I was beginning to think he was taking the role of *protectorate* a little too far. In the past week, a day hadn't gone by when he didn't show up to say something, oftentimes jumping into my body at strange moments, sending every cell in my body dancing with vibration. It was like being plugged into an electrical socket.

You don't like it? His voice was like a whisper on the air, but instead of hearing it, I felt it, thought it, knew it.

I shrugged. "I like it, I just don't think I like the host."

You'll find a better one, the Daemon said with certainty.

"Good. Now, where is Kara?" I let out an exasperated sigh and looked out the half-open office door wondering where my new assistant was. Then I laughed and wondered what people thought of me talking to myself. They probably thought I was a little *off*.

No sooner had I finished wondering where she was when Kara rushed into my office with a pile of disheveled paperwork. "I have it here, but uh, I called that guy. I forget his name…"

I bit my tongue and forced a smile. "That's okay. I just need the contract for *Go-Go-Goetia Incorporated*. I think the guy's name is Simon. Simon Levine."

She dropped half the papers on the floor, her eyes brimming with large, wet tears. "Oh, sorry. You're not going to fire me, are you?"

Not this again, I thought. Kara was the most emotional person I'd ever worked with. She cried at the drop of a hat and thought every little mistake would get her fired. "No, relax. You worry too much."

You'll have to fire her, Lucifuge said matter-of-factly. I thought I detected a bit of amusement in his voice.

"I just don't want you to be mad at me," Kara whimpered.

I fought back a groan and inwardly agreed with Lucifuge because I was going to be mad at her if she kept it up. Being rather thick-skinned and abrasive myself, I rarely cried at work and didn't do well with criers. "No, Kara, I'm not going to be mad. Why do you think that?"

"You were upset about the Evenbright contract."

"Only because I told you how to prepare the documents *four times* and you screwed them up *four times* because you weren't listening and didn't write anything down." Now I was annoyed, and I could hear it in the edge of my own voice. I'd really only agreed to let her work with me because I needed to get things moving and I didn't have the time to hire someone new if I wanted to hit the ground running. Kara looked and sounded reliable in the way Kirk presented her. It was only after the first emotional breakdown I realized I'd made a grave mistake.

She sniffed.

I fought back another groan. Clearly Kara had never been bullied as a child; otherwise, she would have had a far thicker skin. Maybe because she had been the bully? I could only speculate. One thing was for certain though — you couldn't even tell her she'd done something wrong without her crying. She also seemed to take offense when she wasn't hoisted on top of people's shoulders when she did something right. Saying *thank you* and *good job* wasn't good enough. No, there had to be laurels and public acknowledgment in front of a crowd. A high maintenance co-worker if there was one.

"Look," I finally said, "That's water under the bridge. Let's do *Go-Go* and move forward, okay?"

What I really wanted to do was tell her she wasn't working out and tell Kirk I needed to hire someone with a brain, because Kara, even though she did keep my phone calls down to a minimum, did a half-assed job with everything else. Suddenly I had sympathy for all of my previous employers who had kept less than stellar employees long past their usefulness.

"Okay," she sniffed, her clumsy fingers sifting through the contracts.

There was no doubt the contract was out-of-order or attached to something else. "Just leave it and go grab a box of file folders."

She continued trying to sort the mess.

I put my hand out to stop her, scooped up the paperwork and pulled it to my chest. "File folders."

With a sniff and more tears, Kara rushed from my office. I rolled my eyes. Of all the assistants I could have been stuck with, I ended up with the one who tried to manipulate me with tears.

Put an ad in later today. That one is trouble, Lucifuge said.

I nodded and said to the Daemon under my breath, "You ain't kidding."

Let's go downstairs and see what's going on. Lucifuge said. He sounded bored.

I needed a walk, so I set the papers on the edge of my desk, grabbed my coffee cup and my wallet, and slipped out of my office, hoping no one would notice me leaving.

The main secretarial area was empty except for Kirk's assistant, whose back was to me. She was on the phone. Hurrying to the elevator, I pushed the button, thankful when the door opened to an empty lift. I'd made it out unscathed.

I wandered down to the stages and sets, refilled my cup with the bitter coffee at the filming coffee station, and stood at the back of Studio A, watching the latest taping of our Draconian show, unoriginally titled *Draconian Gnosis*.

"Ho Drakon, Ho Megas," came the chant from the front of the room.

I listened to the Draconian ritual and marveled at the artistic beauty of it, even though I was still convinced most of the sigils from that paradigm looked like vagina art. Vagina's in the seals of Sorath and Lucifer even. Someone there really enjoyed that imagery. Either that or *I* was the one obsessed with vaginas.

Lucifuge laughed. *Now, wait for it...*

The high priestess read another long oration. Weren't they supposed to be meditating? I recalled the words of an acquaintance of mine. He was a well-known Chaote named Darren Steele, who hailed from Rhode Island. He'd been on a recent show to discuss Chaos Magick, and we'd been online acquaintances ever since. Our last lunch together, the conversation ended with: "If you're allegedly in deep meditation and are coherent enough to pause and read some fancy oration, you're not doing it right."

We'd agreed on this point, and now, Lucifuge agreed, too. I felt Lucifuge roll my eyes. It seemed that even Daemons found human prattling annoying at times.

The rituals, however, made for gorgeous live television, which is why many magicians at BMN looked to Draconian ritual for ideas to draw their rites out and make them sound all secret-society on camera. Elaborate rituals like this were good for ratings, so no doubt it was also good for selling books and wares. And here I was, a practicing Daemonolatress. Our rituals were effective, certainly, but didn't have nearly as much in the area of monologuing, making them undesirable as theatrical fodder.

You could always dress them up, but their usefulness drops significantly, Lucifuge said. Then he sounded hopeful. *This coffee is terrible. Let's go get some more of that mocha latte from the shop down the street. The Java place.*

You're going to make me fat, I scolded him inwardly.

The Daemon laughed, and when he did, my right eyelid twitched involuntarily. We, and by we I mean me with my attached Daemon passenger, left the studio and started toward the main doors. It was almost noon, and executives often came and went as they wished, so no one batted an eye as I left the building and headed toward *Java, Java.*

My body was buzzing again. *You're burning my body out. Probably going to give me cancer,* I told him. In a way, I was glad we could communicate telepathically because people would have thought I was a crazy woman if I spoke to him aloud out here. In my office, it was one thing. In public, quite another. On the upside, the Daemon stayed out of my body for work tasks, bathing, dressing, and the like. Gods only know what my hair, makeup, and wardrobe choice would have looked like with the Daemon Lucifuge as my stylist. However, he seemed to be bouncing in and out of my body more and more often. When he did, I could usually still see and hear, but I didn't have control over my mouth and limbs. It was a helpless sensation that caused my heart to palpitate and my palms to sweat, though I was becoming more accustomed to it.

I made it to the coffee shop in full control of my faculties and ordered the coffee, then chose an outside table to sit at. The Colorado spring air still had a nip to it. It was sixty-two degrees, with the forecast calling for snow over the weekend and temperatures expected to rise back into the sixties the following Monday. *Springtime in the Rockies*, as the locals were fond of saying.

What an asshole thing to say, Lucifuge said, taking over my body so he could have a sip of the mocha latte. *It's like when it's hot and people say, it sure is hot today,* the Daemon continued. *No shit. Why point out the obvious?*

I laughed just as Lucifuge took a drink, and coffee dribbled from my mouth and straight down onto my brand new, violet blouse with the knotted accents over my chest. *Damn it!* Mike always laughed at how I dribbled food and drink down the front of myself, and while it probably was funny, my blouses ended up stained after one too many mishaps, and I regularly had to replace them as a result. Lesson learned. Apparently, the Daemon hadn't had full control, or he'd been relaxed while having his mocha latte.

Don't laugh this time. I didn't get to taste it, Lucifuge said, making another attempt at sipping the piping hot liquid. After he swallowed and I winced at the pain from my now burnt tongue he said, *this is good.*

"You know, it's a little weird you popping into my body for the occasional mocha latte. While I appreciate you as my protectorate, I'm pretty sure I don't need twenty-four-seven protection," I managed to whisper under my breath.

I need you for more than that, Lucifuge said. *We have to deal with a situation. We Daemons don't possess people without reason, as you well know. We always take willing hosts when we can, and I think you're the perfect person for the job.*

My heart sank. Some days it felt like no one was really your friend - they just wanted something from you. Especially in my new job. All sorts of old acquaintances had resurfaced and begun emailing me, acting like we were old friends once word got out that I was BMN's new programming director.

Now, wait a minute. I like you just the way you are, even if you refuse to help me, Lucifuge assured me before taking another drink from the steaming mug. *You physical beings have no idea what a treat this is.*

What can I help with? I silently asked him.

The Daemon shrugged my shoulders. "In due time," he said aloud in my voice. "I think I'd really like one of those cheeseburgers," he said, my eyes fixed on the burger joint across the street.

Against my will, Lucifuge stood and made his way from quaint coffee shop patio towards the crosswalk, dead set and determined to get a double bacon cheeseburger and a large order of fries. "Don't worry, you can always tell people the devil made you do it," he said in my voice again. Then he chuckled.

Ha, Lucifuge, I thought. *Well played.*

An hour later, with the mustard and ketchup stains barely visible on my once pristine blouse, I sat at my desk Lucifuge-free, waiting on Kara to get my weekly ratings' report put together. From the open office door, I could see her on the other side of the copy room, struggling with the hole punch. Who couldn't work a hole punch? I held back the urge to get up and go help her. Kara had probably been one of the preppy girls in high school, I finally decided. You know the ones - they dated the jocks and belonged to the honor society. Her hairstyle hadn't changed since the mid-eighties, and I wondered then what she thought about having a boss at least fifteen or more years her junior. I was actually surprised Kirk had hired a Wiccan office clerk, and even more surprised a Wiccan had wanted a job working with a cadre of ceremonial magicians and practitioners with darker sensibilities.

Kirk, my boss, stepped into my office, his gaze following mine to my inept office assistant in the windowed copy room across the way.

"I need to hire someone who can use a hole punch," I deadpanned.

"That's not fair. She's a bit slow, but..." Kirk grimaced as he said this. Kara had erroneously hole punched something because she cringed. "Okay, I can move her back to supplies and shipping."

"Thank you. Are you sure she can handle supplies and shipping?" I almost laughed at my own sarcasm. Lucifuge's derision was wearing off on me.

He nodded his head toward Kara. "Is she working on the ratings' report?"

"What's left of it, yes." A spontaneous yawn erupted from me and I stretched.

"Not getting enough sleep?" Kirk stepped into my office and pulled the chair across from my desk away from the wall and closer to me.

"Between my mother and mother-in-law hounding me about the wedding every other day, and struggling to get anything done with my helper here..." *And the Daemon who keeps interrupting for coffee and burger breaks*, I added silently.

"Have Tracy put an ad in for someone new and at the end of the day, and I'll have Tracy inform Kara that she's moving back to shipping. I kind of feel bad for her. She does try..." Kirk gave me a hopeful smile.

Apparently, Kara had used her crying manipulation routine on him, too, but the difference was - he'd fallen for it. "I can understand that. I just need someone quicker on their feet, and Kara isn't that person." I straightened a few file folders and forced a smile when I saw Kara leave the copy room and start heading toward my office. Her eyes were wet and red. She was in tears again. "Here comes the report," I told Kirk in the cheeriest voice I could muster.

Kirk knew me better than that though. He raised an eyebrow and looked expectantly at the doorway as Kara entered with two copies of the Weekly Ratings' report. "Now this has the streaming data in it?"

I gave him a brisk nod. "All two months of it." I stood and took the reports from Kara and handed one of the folders to Kirk. "Thank you, Kara. Could you close the door behind you?"

Kara nodded shyly, sniffed and wiped her eyes, and slipped out of the room, closing the door behind her.

I opened the report to the streaming data page. "It's page thirty-six."

Kirk opened his folder and his face went from relaxed and curious to contorted and confused. "Unholy Goddesses."

I knew exactly what he'd found - a complete mess. Exactly what I'd been dealing with for several weeks now. I held my report out to him and reached across the desk for his. We switched folders and I fought back a groan as I flipped through it. This report folder was out of order, backward, and upside down. She'd hole-punched the wrong side of the pages and possibly dropped them, too.

"How about I take this home with me tonight and look it over this weekend. If I have any questions, we can do lunch next week?" Kirk stood. "I was thinking of leaving early today. Get a game of golf in."

"That's fine with me," I said with a grin, thankful when he left and I was in my office, door closed, all by myself. I finished the afternoon putting my copy of the report back into proper order, then ducked out an hour early so I could miss the water-works of Kara being told she'd been busted back down to supply and shipping clerk. All the while, Lucifuge was silent.

CHAPTER 2

L ucifuge left me alone for the trip home, which included a side trip to the grocery store. I arrived at the house to find Mike sitting at the dining room table with a stack of brochures and papers spread out before him. I didn't pay much attention to what he was looking at, just set down the four bags of groceries on the counter and began unloading them.

"Hey gorgeous," he said with a quick glance in my direction. He was still wearing black slacks and a button-down shirt. He'd been to court earlier in the day to testify against the ringleader in a car theft operation. Usually, he changed when he got home, but whatever was on the table was clearly more interesting than his own comfort. He frowned at the open brochure in front of him. "What do you think about cupcakes instead of an actual wedding cake?"

I pulled a package of hot dogs and buns from one of the bags and set them on the counter next to the toaster. I shrugged. "I haven't really thought about it, but you have to admit that a wedding cake has more of a *presence*."

He laughed. "With pentagrams on it?" He must've known that would get my full attention because when I turned to face him, he was leaning back in the chair, hands folded in front of him on the table, with an expectant look on his face.

I gave him a smirk. "You're serious? You mean, like, an all-out witchy wedding cake?" I should have known curiosity would've gotten the best of me. I left the groceries on the counter and started toward his place at the dining room table. "Why do you ask?"

With one strong hand, Mike reached forward and turned the brochure to face me, then motioned toward it. "Take a look."

A flood of laughter tumbled out of me when I saw the white, butter-frosted cake with pentagrams around the outside. "What is this? Witchy-Cakes-R-Us?"

Mike shook his head, a wide grin on his lips. "My mother. She knows Kenny DeBeers."

"Yikes." It was the only thing I could say. Kenny DeBeers was known for throwing wild theme weddings for some of the wealthiest elites across the country. Every so often, pictures of his parties and their guests would end up on the society pages of major celebrity magazines and large newspapers. I recalled one where all the women wore flesh-colored leotards with faux flowers wrapped around all the bits they didn't want showing. There had been little left to the imagination. "I never agreed to a wedding planner. I was thinking something simple."

With a snort and a *good-luck* look, Mike let out a sigh. "We're dealing with my mother here."

I gave Mike a brief knowing look. Beverly Katz, who had hated me until she found out I was a Daemonolatress, an author, and the programming director of a television network, made it a point to call me at least once a week since she'd learned Mike and I had finally set the date. It was a couple months off yet, which gave her plenty of time to plan, even though Mike and I hadn't asked. My future mother-in-law to be had a sharp tongue, and had no problem insulting me to my face when it suited her.

"You know, we can unite forces and tell her to knock it off." With a lifted brow, he got up and nodded at the stack of brochures and papers. "I'm going to go change out of these clothes. Don't forget the groceries." Then he started toward the stairs.

I sat down in his place and looked at the stack of wedding ideas, then called after him, "Wait, you mean you don't want your mom to plan our wedding?" I heard him groan as he went up the stairs. I laughed.

Beverly had really outdone herself. She had included everything from cake and flower brochures to event space rental flyers. She even had advertisements from local bridal boutiques. Or perhaps she'd paid Kenny DeBeers to collect it all for her. With a forlorn sigh and a glance at our cat, Midnight, I got up and went back to putting away the groceries. Lucifuge butted into my thoughts. *Just go to the courthouse like everyone else.*

"What do you know about relationships and weddings?" I mumbled under my breath.

Midnight meowed and jumped onto the kitchen island. I'd always wanted a cat, but had never had one before, so admittedly, Midnight was a bit spoiled. I let him go where he wanted, figuring he'd alert me to wayward spirits or Daemons in the house, though the cat didn't seem to notice or be bothered by Lucifuge in the least. I took up his dish from the dish drainer and grabbed a can of cat food from the pantry. "Mmm. Ocean fish medley," I told the cat while I opened the can. I'd gotten in the habit of talking to the rambunctious ball of fur and announcing the flavor of food before every evening meal.

The cat rubbed against my legs and spun around at my feet, his meows becoming more urgent as I scooped the food from the container into his bowl. Finally, I set the bowl down on the ground, and the cat immediately went silent as he dug into the meal. You'd have thought I hadn't fed him in years.

The house was quiet, and I cocked my head, listening for any sound of Mike upstairs. My eyes traveled back over to the dining room table and the immense stack of wedding literature. With a heavy sigh, I finished putting away the groceries, purposefully ignoring the intimidating pile on the dining room table, all the while imagining Beverly having a great time planning my wedding.

"Beverly must be having a heyday," I said, then picked up my glass from the counter and filled it with water. I took a few sips of the tepid liquid and set it back on the counter and decided I should go upstairs and change into something more comfortable. If I was going to look at wedding brochures, there was no point being dressed up for it.

I found Mike laying on the bed in a pair of sweatpants and nothing else with his hands folded over his stomach, eyes closed. "You're opting for a nap?"

"Just trying to unwind from my day," he said. "So, what's for dinner?"

"Funny, I was going to ask you the same thing." The truth was I wasn't all that hungry. The burger from lunch sat heavy on my stomach and the thought of food made me queasy. "I guess I'm not that hungry."

"Yeah, I had a big lunch too. Maybe I'll just have a yogurt." He opened one eye and looked at me suspiciously.

I laughed at the yogurt bit. Mike didn't look like the yogurt type. He was tall, dark, handsome, and muscular, and anyone who looked at him would've taken him for meat and potatoes man. "Fair enough." Now he'd opened his eyes and was giving me a quizzical look. "What?"

"Did you do something different with your hair?" He closed his eyes again.

"No, why? Does it look bad?" Nothing makes a woman feel more self-conscious than when her man starts making strange, random comments about her looks. My hand went to my head, and I ran it through the length of my hair, wondering if the grease from the burger at somehow seeped out of my scalp.

"I don't know. You seem to have a glow about you." He didn't open his eyes.

I began to undress, throwing my clothes into the laundry basket, silently patting myself on the back each time an article of clothing made it in. Today was one of those days I would've been proud to be on my own basketball team. "I suppose I should go back downstairs and go through that wedding stuff, because I have no doubt your mother's going to ask me about it, and I don't want to be caught without an answer."

Mike laughed.

"So, you want to come down and go through it with me?" I slipped on a pair of sweatpants and a T-shirt and climbed onto the bed next to him.

He turned to me and opened his eyes. "Isn't wedding planning supposed to be the woman's job?"

"So, you mean to tell me you would be happy if I chose lemon cake and hot pink for cummerbunds and bridesmaid dresses?" I said that knowing that he hated both lemon cake and hot pink.

He chuckled and took my hand into his. "I know you better than that. You don't have such crappy taste. I trust you."

It was my turn to laugh, partly because he was right that I had much better taste, but also because I knew that when it came to big events, Mike just liked to show up. He didn't want to have to plan it. "Well good. You know your mother will be doing most of the planning anyway, right? After all, it's not every day her first and only son gets married."

"Of that, I have no doubt. I think the more we let her plan, the happier she will be."

I groaned, drew in a deep breath, and let out a heavy sigh. He was right. Beverly was the one who wanted to plan a big wedding. Mike and I, we would have been happy to elope. Whenever we were invited to a wedding, we always made plans to duck out early or hide in a corner to avoid human interaction as much as possible. Smalltalk was exhausting for the both of us. "Next thing you know she'll want to name our children," I said, sitting up.

Mike chuckled again, not letting go of my hand. "So, you do want kids, then?"

I shrugged. "Maybe one. Two if I'm bored. What about you?" Sure, we discussed kids in the past, but getting married seem to make the idea more concrete, which warranted more serious discussion.

"That works for me." That was all he said. He let go of my hand, a smile still on his lips. "Enjoy my mother's crazy antics."

"You're not getting out of it that easily. You know your mother is going to want your input at some point. I'm not going to argue with her. That's your job." I got up, padded across the room, and glanced back at him on the bed, then made my way back downstairs.

The cat had finished eating and was now lounging on the counter stretched out licking a paw. He scarcely glanced at me as I entered the room. "Lazy cat," I said. "Come over and help me pick out some things."

I laughed at myself for anthropomorphizing the cat and having a conversation with it. I wondered then, if we had gotten a miniature pig, if the pig would have understood me any better. Pigs were supposed to be smart - smarter than cats anyway. That made me wonder if Beverly would bring Jodie, her pet miniature pig, to the wedding. "Maybe Jodie could be the ring bearer," I said, laughing to myself.

The insurmountable pile of wedding brochures stared at me from the table, and I immediately felt overwhelmed.

One piece of paper at a time, Lucifuge said in my mind. He was back. At least I wouldn't have to go through flowers, cakes, and wedding dresses by myself. However, I was also pretty certain that Daemons didn't make good wedding planners. *Give me half a chance,* Lucifuge said.

I smiled and shook my head and sat down at the table leaning on my elbows. The brochure on top had nothing but flowers and it. I didn't know much about flowers, and unless they had some sort of magical or poisonous properties, I really didn't have much interest. I grew some odd houseplants like my mandrake, and I had some belladonna in the backyard greenhouse. The truth of the matter was that I couldn't tell a peony from a buttercup, and I had no idea what an anemone was. Most of the colors were pastel, and me and pastels didn't get along.

Those white ones are pretty, Lucifuge chimed in as I flipped through the pages of lilies and hydrangeas, prairie gentian and cape jasmine, and by the time I reached the final page I'd seen so many white, pink, and purple flowers that I was pretty sure Beverly would know what to do. Sometimes it was just easier to delegate.

"We'll just let Beverly deal with that," I said to Lucifuge, setting the brochure off to the side.

Go with those white ones, Lucifuge responded.

I let out a heavy sigh and folded over the page with the Cape Jasmine on it. Then I set that brochure off to the side and sifted through the pile until I found what appeared to be a book of cakes.

Cake! Lucifuge pushed closer to the forefront of my mind.

I laughed at the Daemon's response. "Yes, cake. Now, this is serious," I told him. I opened the brochure. This bakery was serious because they had a full fifty-seven page, full-color catalog filled with various options for nothing but wedding cakes. The truth was I didn't care how big the cake was because the guest list would determine that. I was only interested in the type of frosting and the type of cake. That was where my expertise was. I was one hell of a cake tester.

I'd like to try some cake, Lucifuge said, even more enthusiastic now. *I don't think I've tried cake yet.*

"Speak for yourself," I mumbled under my breath. "I eat cake all the time." Then I giggled.

Funny, Lucifuge deadpanned. *We should go to a cake tasting.*

I laughed. I imagined me and Beverly going to the bakery to sample cakes and Lucifuge commenting on everyone. Then I realized in abject horror that Lucifuge could, if he wanted, take over my body and taste the cake with Beverly - with me sitting on the sidelines watching. No matter what happened, I couldn't let my future mother-in-law have an outing with the Daemon. Especially since Lucifuge wasn't one for manners or tact.

That's not fair. I can be tactful. Then the Daemon went silent.

In the very back of the catalog was a list of all the flavors and frosting types that they could do for any cake. The list spanned two pages, and I winced. There was a lot more to this wedding planning stuff than I realized. I set the cake book aside, figuring Beverly and I, and probably Lucifuge, would have to go taste. Otherwise, I wasn't sure I could make up my mind.

"Whatever happened to the good old days when you only had the choice of vanilla, chocolate, and yellow? Maybe with some kind of fruit filling, or cream. Or when everything was butter frosting?" I asked aloud. I shook my head at the list. "Look at this. Now they have nuts, fruit, cream, and about seventy-five different flavors. Ten types of chocolate alone, if not more."

That's good though, right? Lucifuge asked.

"No. It's a pain in the ass. So much for making choices." I set that brochure aside.

Next on the stack was a sampling of wedding invitation stationery. I would've been happy to have simply printed off invitations on our laser printer and shove them into number ten envelopes, using an address database and printable labels to deal with the mailing.

"I could probably farm that job off to one of the secretaries at the office," I mused aloud. Then I realized there was no way I'd find time to pull out my calligraphy set and make out each invitation individually. That, too, would have to be hired out. I shuffled through the stationary until I found an invitation I liked. It was a small three-by-five card in cream-colored linen with gilded lettering in a cursive font.

Elegant and simple. A good choice, Lucifuge said.

I nodded in agreement and set that aside because that was a choice I *could* make.

Finally, there were several brochures for different wedding venues. I set them on the table in front of me and thumbed through them.

Something in the mountains would be nice, Lucifuge quipped.

"Yeah, but this is a decision that will be dictated by the number of guests." I pulled the brochures for the three event centers in the mountains. "Let's narrow it to one of these three. Then once my mother gets her list together, and Beverly gets her list together, we'll at least have a general headcount."

Agreed, Lucifuge said. *Who will be conducting the ceremony?*

"Mike and I already agreed to have the high priest of Beverly's coven conduct the ceremony," I told the Daemon.

"That made her happy. My concern is my family doesn't know of my Daemonic leanings."

That should be… interesting. Lucifuge chuckled.

I let out a nervous laugh. "You don't know the half of it."

Then tell me about it. I could feel Lucifuge waiting for me to tell him.

I looked around to make sure Mike wasn't within earshot, not wanting to have to explain why I was talking to myself. Then I kept my voice low. "My parents are relatively low maintenance. Especially with the whole wedding thing. They like Mike, or rather that he has a respectable job. Anyone who is military or police – they approve of. They also think it's a prestige thing that he's a detective, kind of like Beverly likes the prestige of me being an author and program director at the BMN."

I see. So, what is the problem other than your spiritual leaning? I could almost envision the Daemon lifting an eyebrow at me.

"It's the social class thing," I whispered. "My family is working middle class, which is a huge contrast to Mike's well-to-do family. Beverly's friends and family are far more affluent, and I'm not so sure I like the idea of those two worlds colliding at my wedding."

Lucifuge chuckled. *At least it will be entertaining.*

"Great, thanks." I could feel the Daemon's amusement web its way through me. I carefully set aside all of the venue brochures, with my two favorites on top. "No doubt Beverly will approve of all the things I chose, considering she was the one who put all of these brochures together."

Probably, Lucifuge agreed.

"At least she's paying for it," I whispered.

Ah, yes. Money is always an issue for you physical beings, he said.

"Well, usually the bride's family pays," I explained. "We were going to pay for everything ourselves, but when Beverly heard, she insisted on footing the bill. Mike gave in because he didn't want to fight with his mom. He'd never hear the end of it if he turned her down."

And how do you feel about that? the Daemon asked.

This was starting to feel like a therapy session, but I went with it. It felt good to get it off my chest. "Considering the expense of the wedding Beverly wanted us to have, and that most of this stuff is way outside our budget, I'm happy to let her foot the bill."

Human pair bonding rituals seem unnecessarily complicated, the Daemon said. I could tell he wasn't finished with the thought, so I kept quiet. *I can understand the cake and the mingling of families, but I'm not so sure I understand the flowers and the choice of location. Do these things matter?*

I thought I heard Mike coming down the stairs, so I pressed my mouth shut. *The location,* I told Lucifuge silently, *is so you can fit all the family members together so they can mingle. The flowers are for decoration. We haven't gotten into the wardrobe yet.*

It matters what you wear? While the Daemon understood a great many things, it was clear I would have to explain why physical beings were so obsessed with physical things.

Some people believe you should dress in a certain way to celebrate big occasions, I explained.

I see, Lucifuge said. *It appears you find all of this tiring. Is it being forced upon you?*

If I had it my way, I would choose something simpler, I admitted.

*But is this not **your** pair-bonding?* Perhaps the Daemon understood more than I gave him credit for.

Yes, but for the sake of family peace and tranquility, I am willing to sacrifice what I want to make others happy. I swallowed the lump that was beginning to form in my throat.

I see, he said again. In that moment, I wished that I could see his thoughts like he could see mine. I wanted to know if the Daemon was judging me.

If making others happy makes you happy, then I suppose it's fine. Lucifuge went silent then.

You still haven't told me why you're here. Why you keep taking over my body and interrupting my thoughts. It's hard enough trying to plan this wedding and deal with my mother-in-law and my job without throwing you into the mix. I hoped I didn't come off as rude, but there was no sense in holding back how I really felt. He would have seen through a lie anyway.

I need your help with something, but for now, you need a protectorate.

Help with what?

The Daemon changed the subject. *Right now, you need protection from your own anxiety. I can help with that.*

Help for what? I repeated.

In due time, Lucifuge said. *Now is not the right moment.*

With an irritated, reluctant sigh, I dropped it and went back to sorting the brochures into the appropriate piles until the table before me was clear. I didn't even notice Mike standing behind me.

"You went through that pretty quickly." He sat down in the chair next to me and looked at my carefully cultivated piles. He started to reach for one, and I put out my hand to stop him.

"Don't mess up my stacks. It took me a half hour to go through all of this. Let's just leave them here until your mother shows up. Half the stuff I'll probably let her deal with anyway. Plus, things I like are on the top, and I don't want them to get lost. I can't choose a cake size because I don't know how many people will be there. I can't choose a venue because again, I have no idea how many people are coming. That sounds more like your mother's Department. With flowers, I have no idea. They all look too dainty and virginal for me." My voice had raised in pitch and a pain went through my chest. I took a deep breath. It had been years since I'd had an anxiety attack, since college.

At that, Mike laughed. "We could get you a bouquet of black flowers if you like, if that's more to your speed. You don't have to do what my mother suggests, you know. I know we both would just rather let her deal with it, but this is our wedding."

With raised eyebrows, I turned to him and couldn't help but smile. "Well, that's a change of attitude. Only forty minutes ago we were both talking about allowing your mother to deal with it."

He shrugged and gave me a sheepish grin. "We say that but you and I both know that at some point we're going to have to stand up to her so you can have the wedding you want."

"If I had the wedding I wanted, it would have consisted of a visit to the Justice of the Peace and a barbecue at your mom's estate. You and I both know that is not going to fly with your mother, and it's probably not going to fly with mine. Better off accepting our fate and keeping the peace." My shoulders slumped.

This time, we both laughed. Mike got up to get himself some yogurt, and I got up and went to the living room to indulge in some light reading before calling it a night. Since tomorrow was Saturday, I fully expected to find Beverly at my door bright and early.

CHAPTER 3

I woke to find Mike standing over me with his nine-millimeter Glock pointed directly at my forehead. "What the fuck, babe?" I scrambled backward and upright.

"Liz?" Mike slowly lowered the gun, his eyes not leaving mine. "Is that you?"

"Yeah! What the hell?" I slid out of bed and inched my way toward the bathroom, my eyes not leaving his, nor the gun in his hands. "This is why I don't like guns. If you ever go crazy and shoot me - help me gods - I will haunt your ass. Why did I wake up with you pointing a gun at me?"

Mike's thumb clicked the safety on the gun and his arm visibly relaxed and lowered to his side. "You don't remember any of that?"

"That's not an answer," I said, standing in the doorway to the bathroom, my heart thumping in my chest. "Why were you pointing a gods-damned gun at my head?" I paused to draw in a breath. "Any of what?"

"It wasn't you." He lowered his eyes. "You shoved me and woke me up and started talking about the human race, politics, burgers, and cake. But it wasn't you. Your eyes were red." It must've been the look on my face because Mike paused and narrowed his eyes. "Is there something you want to tell me?"

A wave of fear and guilt washed over me. "I didn't want you to worry," I said, not bothering to explain.

"Liz?" He lifted an eyebrow and let out a heavy sigh. "What aren't you telling me?"

"Gods forbid I ever try to throw you a surprise party. You'd find out," I said half under my breath. "I don't know how I thought I could keep this from you." My sigh emerged as more of a shudder, adrenaline still racing through my veins.

He lifted his left eyebrow and took on that detective-interrogation-tone. "Okay. Start at the top."

"Back at the Cloven Hoof, when Monica Niel was trying to force me to drink poison, I invoked Lucifuge for strength. This feeling went through me like nothing I'd ever experienced, and when Monica and I got into that fight, I felt like I had superhuman strength. I mean, I knocked her across the room. I hit her so hard she knocked down a few displays as she went. For a few weeks after that, I kept hearing, in my mind's eye, the Daemon talking to me. Then, he started taking over my body on occasion." I cringed, waiting for Mike's response. He moved over to the bed and sat down, setting the gun next to him on the rumpled comforter.

I wasn't sure how to break the tension in the room. "Well, at least we know that if I'm Daemon possessed, the Daemon has good reason. They don't usually take a human host unless they have something important they need to do."

"Like wake me up to talk about politics, humanity, and junk food?" Mike seemed to mull this around in his brain for a moment before finally asking, "Has the Daemon told you what it wants?"

"I've asked a couple of times, and he keeps telling me that he'll let me know in due time." The aggravation in my voice caused Mike's expression to soften. I continued, "He keeps stepping into my body at really inconvenient times to partake in junk food and mocha lattes." I said. I stepped into the bathroom and looked into the mirror, expecting to find tired eyes with dark circles. Instead, I looked refreshed and my face felt dewy.

It's all those moisturizing Daemons, Lucifuge quipped.

"Great," I said to myself in the mirror, then to Mike who was still sitting on the edge of the bed, "So what's next? I go see a psychiatrist to make sure I'm not crazy or developing split personalities?"

"Actually, I was thinking maybe we should call Alyssa and see if she and Gabe will perform an exorcism," Mike said.

I poked my head out the bathroom doorway and gave him a quizzical look. "Seriously? Are you sure you're not the one who's possessed?"

He still didn't laugh, even though there was plenty of humor in the situation - from my view, anyway. He got up and went to the nightstand on his side of the bed, grabbing his phone.

"It's five o'clock in the morning. Alyssa will kill you if you wake her up," I warned.

"Liz, you may not be possessed right now, but you have a Daemon playing around in your body. We have too much going on. We have my mother and a wedding planner coming over today, and I'll be damned if some Daemon is going to possess you and start making decisions about our wedding plans." Mike tapped the phone screen and put it up to his ear.

"He promised he wouldn't possess me during wedding planning, except for the cake tasting part. He really wants to try cake, and I kind of told him that would be okay," I said, wincing even as I mentioned it.

"With red eyes and all?" he asked, wide-eyed. Then his attention turned to the phone, or rather who just answered. "Hey, Gabe. It's Mike. Sorry to call you so early but I have a situation here. It seems Liz is possessed, and my mother will be here in five hours with a wedding planner."

There was a pause and Mike said, "It's not funny, man. It's freaky as shit. If my mother finds out…"

That is when a strange surge of energy coursed through me. My mind was shoved aside as the Daemon took over. Apparently, Lucifuge had a thing or two to say about being exorcised. I could feel the Daemon in every part of my psyche.

When I spoke next it was my voice, but lower, deeper, not me. "You don't have to exorcise me. I promise I won't show up except for the cake," Lucifuge said.

Mike stood, looking around for the gun.

"Relax," the Daemon said.

"I can't relax while you're possessing my girlfriend. You can't tell me the only reason you're doing this is that you want some goddamn cake. I'll bake you a fucking cake if it means you'll leave us alone." Mike started toward Lucifuge. I could see everything going on, but I had no control over my own body.

"Fine," the Daemon said, holding out my hands defensively, causing Mike to stop dead in his tracks. "I'm here to remove someone dangerous and I needed a body to do.it in."

Mike's face contorted into horrified shock - an expression I'd never seen him wear. "You're going to kill someone using Liz's body and then leave her to take the murder rap?"

"Well, when you put it that way, it sounds terrible. However, I assure you that all of humankind will be thankful for what I need to do. Besides, I never said I'd have to kill anyone." The Daemon shrugged my shoulders. "Now, how can I go about getting some cheese fries?"

Mike slowly lifted the phone back to his ear. "Are you hearing this?" Then he tapped the screen, presumably hanging up.

The Daemon started toward the door, his destination firm in my mind. The kitchen. The cat didn't even look up when he passed by, sound asleep in a nearby chair, completely unbothered by everything going on.

"We don't have cheese fries," Mike said, shoving past me and leading the way to the kitchen. This time, he didn't have his gun, for which I was thankful. How he thought a gun would solve the problem of a supernatural being inhabiting my body was something we would have to discuss later.

"Very well," Lucifuge said with a sigh. "I suppose I can settle for ice cream. Or maybe a cheeseburger."

"We're going to finish this conversation. That's what's going to happen," Mike said over his shoulder as he started down the stairs.

Humans, Lucifuge said so only I could hear him. *You and your morality, and refusal to accept that some of your kind should be destroyed for the good of many.*

We have laws, I told him telepathically. *We put those who kill others in prison.*

Unless the killing is sanctioned by those in power, he countered.

Fair point, I said.

Oblivious to our conversation, Mike flicked on the overhead light and turned to me. He had that look in his eye that said he was going to be practical. I wasn't disappointed; it was his practicality that I loved about him. "We need to figure out how we're going to solve your problem and mine in an amicable way. I want you out of my fiancée, and you want someone dangerous taken off the streets. That is my job, you know."

"Why do you think I chose Elizabeth?" Lucifuge, in my body, started toward the fridge.

I'm never going to be able to fit into my wedding dress, I complained inwardly.

"Don't worry, I'll make sure you'll be able to fit in your dress," Lucifuge said aloud.

"What?" Mike asked.

"Elizabeth is complaining that I'm eating too much food and she won't be able to fit into her wedding dress." There was no hint of emotion in the Daemon's voice. Though I thought I felt the Daemon roll my eyes.

"So, she's in there? She can hear what's going on?" Mike said over to the counter and turned on the coffee pot.

"Of course, she's in here. She's not being harmed at all. When she's awake, she can hear everything we're talking about." Lucifuge opened the refrigerator door and peered in, frowning. "There's nothing in here that I want. Let's go get burgers."

Mike ignored the Daemon's suggestion. "So, you chose Elizabeth because I work in law enforcement."

The Daemon nodded and turned to Mike while closing the refrigerator. "Partly, yes. Her body is strong enough to hold me, and she's willing. Elizabeth and I need to infiltrate a cult so we can get close to its leader. You will be in charge of running things from the outside to make sure we deal with this person accordingly. Though killing him would be much easier. However, that probably wouldn't solve the bigger issue," the Daemon said nonchalantly. I could tell he was amused, but I had no idea why.

Mike, still narrow-eyed, bit his lower lip. "Fine. First thing I need is the person's name and why he or she poses such a danger. I can't run around arresting people for things they haven't done."

"We will get you the evidence." Lucifuge let out an irritated sigh. "I just need to be able to get close enough to see the evidence for myself, so I can share that evidence with you." The Daemon helped himself to a coffee mug.

"Enough evidence that you were willing to use Liz's body to commit murder?" Mike asked, grabbing himself a coffee cup.

Lucifuge was exasperated, I could feel it. Just short of snorting, the Daemon let out another exaggerated sigh and said, "I never said I was going to kill anyone. You just thought that's what I meant. I found it too amusing to correct you."

"What did you mean, then?" Mike poured his coffee first, then stepped out of the way so the Daemon could get his cup as well.

"I was simply saying that if it was required of me, I would remove the threat. I never said I would use Liz's hands to commit murder. That's ridiculous. I am a Daemon after all. I can kill a man without needing physical hands to do so." The Daemon generously added cream and sugar to his coffee, then took it over to the dining room table, and sat down.

Mike followed. "Then why do you need Liz at all?"

Good point, I thought.

The Daemon leaned back in the chair and tipped my head sideways, looking at Mike through what I could only imagine were red-tinged eyes. "I need to be able to get close enough to the guy. The only way I can do that is with a human host."

Mike leaned forward on the table, forearms planted firmly. He narrowed his eyes and bit his lower lip. "So, tell me everything you know about the person we're trying to catch. All the details, leaving nothing out."

Lucifuge and I relaxed, and the Daemon took a long drink of coffee and scowled a bit. "This isn't good, not like the mocha latte."

"You're stalling," Mike said. He was obviously annoyed.

"Fine, get me the laptop, and I'll show you. Everything you need to know is in an email that was sent to one of the Black Magick Network's email accounts. No one has seen it yet." Lucifuge drank more coffee. For not liking it, he'd already drunk almost the entire cup.

Mike went over to the small desk we kept in the dining room. The laptop was there, along with all our bills and junk mail. We affectionately called it *the shit collector.* He brought the computer back, opened it, and set it in front of Lucifuge.

I could feel the Daemon probing my mind for the username and password as he effortlessly plucked it from my memory and typed it in. Surprisingly, he wasn't a bad typist either, though, just like common phrases and language, I suspected he was drawing from my skill set and not his own.

"No one ever uses this email. It's a catch-all for the crazies who write to the network," the Daemon explained. It was true. We did keep several email addresses just like that to catch all of the unwanted hate and religious email. "I'll read it to you."

I heard Mike move to stand over my shoulder so he could see for himself what Lucifuge was about to read. I read along as well.

"It has come to the attention of the *Dark Diocese* that you do not support our legions. Please know that it is dangerous for you, magically or otherwise, to slander, disrespect, or otherwise take any action, in public or private against us. We acknowledge that you have your own petty beliefs. You have that right. Just remember – the Dark Diocese is Legion, and we are many. We are powerful and will not hesitate to seek revenge and punish those who cross us. Even if you wish to remain silent, it would be wise to spread this proclamation amongst those weak-minded individuals who follow you. By the word of our Dark Pope, Drakaris Deathspell. By the word of our Dark Warlord, Sethial." Lucifuge paused and looked back over my shoulder at Mike who wore an *are you kidding me* expression.

Mike snorted. "It sounds like one of those role-playing games."

The Daemon nodded. "It appears they have used something called a *Monster Manual* for their mythology. Something about *dark elves,* whatever those are. But that doesn't make their idiocy any less dangerous."

We should respond, I thought, chuckling to myself. *But what if they know who I am?* I asked.

"Undoubtedly, they know of you, and if they've done their research, they know you're part of the Black Magick Network, but none of them have seen your face," Lucifuge said. "Besides, I can make you look like anyone I choose. I am a Daemon, after all."

Mike gave me a weird look.

"I'm talking to Liz," Lucifuge clarified as he sifted through more email. He clicked on one where the subject read, *Ancient Sumerian Daemonolatry Manuscript Uncovered.*

I read it: *We have uncovered an ancient Daemonolatry manuscript that will prove that we are the only true traditional Daemonolaters, and all others are false.*

Lucifuge laughed. "This ancient manuscript was written in English last month, and then they just highlighted all of it and changed it to an Anglo-Saxon Rune font. Humans. Amusing." Nothing else took the Daemon's, fancy so he closed the laptop.

"Great, yet another threat from another cult," Mike said, this time with a tinge of worry in his voice. I knew what he was thinking. He was recalling the last email I'd gotten from a strange, ridiculous cult with an equally stupid name. The woman running that one had been no other than Monica Niel, serial killer extraordinaire, using human blood to make her infamous *Blood of Saturn*. I learned the hard way that even the ridiculous cults could be dangerous.

When you share your body with a Daemon, keeping your thoughts to yourself is impossible. Lucifuge nodded. "They are dangerous. This Drakaris Deathspell believes he's going to bring about Armageddon, and he is having his followers collect materials to make bombs, which he plans to set off in major cities across the United States. He's also willing to force his followers to kill themselves rather than be caught by authorities."

Mike was dead quiet, almost too quiet. Then the doorbell rang. Without a single word, Mike stood and went to the door, leaving me and the Daemon alone.

This sounds like a job for the FBI or something, I thought. *Homeland security maybe?*

Perhaps, Lucifuge said telepathically. *However, I need you to go into the cult so I can have a talk with them. Especially the leader.*

Who takes on the moniker Drakaris Deathspell, anyway? I asked, amused.

The Daemon shrugged my shoulders. *We could discuss the psychological profile of this individual, but that would bore us both.*

I could hear voices at the front door, and footfalls coming toward the kitchen, rushing in fact. In a strange jolt, Lucifuge disappeared, and I was left standing in my own body able to speak and move. Even though I had not been deprived of oxygen, I drew in a deep breath as if it was the first time I'd breathed in hours.

"He's in her right now," Mike was telling Gabe.

I could tell Alyssa and Gabe had rushed to dress because Alyssa was wearing pink sweatpants, and Gabe's t-shirt was inside out. With a crinkled nose, I cringed at the sweatpants. "Those aren't very Satanic, Liss."

Her eyes moved from me to Mike and Gabe, then down at the pink sweatpants. "What's wrong with them?"

"They're…" I felt a whoosh and fell into the darkness of my mind as Lucifuge slid right back into my mind through my crown chakra.

"Bright," Lucifuge finished in a far more dignified tone than was my usual demeanor. "So, are these your associates, Michael?"

"Yeah. Alyssa, and Gabriel." Mike's voice was distant.

I felt my mind tumbling backward, deeper into myself than I had ever gone before while the Daemon possessed me. Momentary panic and terror ran through me, and I felt a firm force pull me forward.

"I have to leave Elizabeth's body for a while. She is weak and tired. I should limit the contact as much as possible until we're inside the cult." The Daemon began to withdraw, and I could feel the pressure on the top of my head.

"I still have questions," Mike said. He sounded pissed.

"I can use her body." Lucifuge nodded toward Alyssa.

"Why not me?" Gabe asked.

"You're not suitable. Too defiant," Lucifuge said, again lacking emotion.

"No," Alyssa said. I could imagine her standing firm, defiant. "I am not a suitable host right now."

"Oh," the Daemon said knowingly, as if he'd just learned a secret.

I caught a glimpse of what he saw, but it was too brief for it to register at that moment.

Lucifuge withdrew a little more. "I will answer all of your questions soon. In the meantime, the email is your first clue. I suppose you can track things like that?"

"Of course," Mike said.

"Good." With that - Lucifuge withdrew and a dull thudding started at the top of my head and crept down my neck like firm tendrils, squeezing my head like a vice as it went. Just when I was about to cry out, the pain was gone. I found myself reaching out to steady myself from a dizzying roll, and I felt arms grabbing me. Light assaulted my eyes, and I squinted at the dim light of the kitchen as if I were staring into the sun.

Alyssa touched my elbow. "Are you okay?"

"You saw it, then?" Mike asked them. His need to validate the experience to ensure his own sanity was clear in his voice.

"The extreme change in demeanor..." Alyssa started.

Gabe threw his hands up. "I don't know, Liss. The red eyes were a dead giveaway."

A nervous laugh emerged from Alyssa. "Yeah, and that."

Mike steadied me and led me to a chair at the table, where he helped me sit. "So, what do we do now?"

He looked tired, his face creased with worry.

I slumped into the chair, thankful to be back in my body even though every pore screamed for sleep. "You have your internet people look into the email and find out where it came from. Maybe tomorrow, after wedding plans, we can do some online research and see what Deathspell has been up to in recent months. In the meantime, I need sleep because I have to take care of your mom and the wedding planner in a few hours."

No one in the room responded, so I stood and willed myself from the room and up the stairs to the bedroom, feeling their eyes following me until my feet hit the top landing. I paused before going into the bedroom, holding onto the railing for support, and even though I shouldn't have, I eavesdropped on their conversation.

At first, I just heard murmurs until Mike finally asked, clearly upset, "What am I supposed to do now?"

"It's been my experience with this sort of thing that you should let the Daemon do what it needs to do. He'll leave on his own. If we attempt to remove him, he may not be happy about it. At best, he'd leave and never show up again. At worst - he'd leave, and Liz would need to find a different spiritual path," Alyssa said clearly. I could only imagine the thoughtful, concerned look on her face. Then they lowered their voices again. I gave up trying to listen after a few minutes and went into the bedroom, promptly throwing myself onto the bed, the darkness finding me straightaway.

CHAPTER 4

I woke Saturday to the sound of Beverly's voice trailing up the stairs. "Go get Elizabeth. It's almost eleven! Who sleeps that late? Really?"

"Mom, she didn't sleep well last night," Mike started.

"From the looks of it, neither did you. She can go to bed early tonight. This is important, Michael. Get her up. Kenny charges by the hour," Beverly said, her voice shrill and rising in pitch.

The voice that followed was foreign to me, and I could only guess it was Kenny DeBeers - wedding planner to the well-to-do. "That I do. I'll set up on the dining room table."

I heard Mike's footfalls ascend the stairs and I groaned, half expecting Lucifuge to show up and offer commentary, but he didn't.

There was a knock on the door, and I turned my head toward it just in time to see Mike duck his dark head of hair into the cool, muted light of the bedroom. "You up?

"Barely. Your mother has a voice that could break glass." I forced myself into a sitting position, wanting to drop back onto the pillow and drift to sleep again.

He laughed. That was one of the many things I loved about Mike. No matter what dangers we faced, or how strange things got in our relationship, he always seemed to keep his sense of humor. He lowered his voice. "Well, you better get up and get dressed, forgo the shower, and get down there. The wedding guy is flamboyant and likes to touch my arm. He's a close talker."

I furrowed my brow. "Close talker?"

Mike stepped into the room and closed the door behind him. "Yeah - he got five inches from my face and started talking, and when I backed up, he stepped forward."

"Hmm," I said. Mike wasn't the type to be easily intimidated. "What did his breath smell like?"

"Cheese," Mike said without skipping a beat.

I broke into laughter. Mike just shook his head and left the room. The thought of a flamboyant wedding planner with cheese breath was enough to spur me into the bathroom to put myself together and get dressed, before heading down to rescue Mike from something most men hated — wedding planning.

Ten minutes later I bounded down the stairs in a pair of sweatpants and a tank top - no shoes. Beverly, Kenny DeBeers, now affectionately known as Cheese Breath, and Mike were all sitting around the dining room table. A look of relief washed over Mike's face. Whether it was merely because I was there, or my eyes didn't have that red tinge of Lucifuge - or both - I didn't know. I made a mental note to ask him about it later.

Beverly gave me the once over and sighed. "We might be leaving later to go to the cake shop."

Don't say the C word, I thought as momentary panic ran through me, but thankfully, Lucifuge didn't show up demanding cake. "That's fine. I can run upstairs and throw on a pair of jeans and a sweater. It will take me all of five minutes."

Beverly and I had our ups and downs. She was from a well-to-do family and had all the graces of a lady. Notice I didn't say they were *good* graces. Beverly had a barbed tongue. Looking down her nose at others seemed to be a favored past time. Mike's mom and I hadn't always seen eye-to-eye, and she hadn't really accepted me as Mike's girlfriend until she learned that I was high up on the Black Magick Network's payroll and was a moderately known occult personality. She'd revealed to me in recent months that she was a witch, too, a fact that even Mike hadn't known up to that point. So that's where me and Beverly's relationship stood - somewhere between friends and enemies - and that seemed to change from day-to-day depending on her mood. While she no longer thought I was lowly and her son was too good for me, economically speaking, she still disliked my unrefined mannerisms and fashion sense, and frequently called me out on both.

With a shrug, Beverly turned her attention to Kenny and gave him a pleasant smile. "So where should we start?"

"Flowers," Kenny said, immediately grabbing the brochure I'd managed to thumb through the night before. He held it in his thick, pudgy hand, opened it, and then wide-eyed and inquisitive asked, "Did you have time to go through this?"

I noticed he didn't look at Mike, and Mike leaned back in his chair as if to become one with the counter and wall behind him so that Cheese Breath wouldn't pay him any attention. "Yes, I looked at it. I thought I would ask Beverly what she thought. I don't know much about flowers."

The ball was in her court. I lifted an eyebrow and gave Beverly my it's-your-move look.

With a pleased-as-punch-smile, my soon-to-be mother-in-law said, "I think the cape jasmine is beautiful. So delicate and refined. Don't you think these are darling, Elizabeth?"

She held out the brochure to me in thin hands with a perfect French manicure. I noted the page I'd marked with Lucifuge's help the night before and nodded. "That's why I marked the page. I liked it. Jasmine is great. It smells nice, too." That constituted everything I knew about jasmine right there.

"Let's go with the cape jasmine, buttercups, and hydrangeas," she said to Kenny, who was furiously scribbling notes in his notebook. Then she turned back to me. "Does that sound good, dear?"

"It sounds fabulous," I said, trying to muster some excitement. I knew I fell flat when everyone at the table paused and glanced at me. I smiled wider. Mike chuckled.

For the first time since I'd sat down, I really looked at Kenny DeBeers. He had a pleasant, round face and wire-rimmed glasses, and wore a pale green button-down shirt and black slacks. Round and stout, he gave me an expectant look, "Now, have we decided on a venue?" His questioning gaze shifted from me to Beverly, then toward Mike.

"We don't really know how many people we have yet. My mother hasn't sent me the list, and I don't know how many people are on Mike's list," I said, drawing Cheese Breath's gaze from Mike, who looked horrified. "Does anyone want some coffee? I could really use a cup."

"I'll have some tea," Beverly said. "Earl Grey, if you have it."

I did. My tea selection was almost as vast as my coffee varieties. If it was caffeinated, it had a place in my coffee and tea cupboard. "Mr. DeBeers?"

"I'd love some tea as well. What kind do you have?"

Mike groaned. "You'll have to go take a look in the tea cupboard. She collects them."

In a few awkward moves, Kenny DeBeers hoisted his stout frame from the chair and made his way to the tea cupboard with me. I began pulling out boxes of tea. Herbal tea, black tea, oolong, and green tea. My favorite was a blend of black tea with orange pekoe. He chose green tea.

I took my time getting the coffee and tea sorted, and by the time I sat back down, we had already decided on the invitation stationery that I liked. What we couldn't agree on were how many bridesmaids and groomsmen. I did not have an abundance of friends, and while Alyssa was my obvious choice for maid of honor, I didn't have any girlfriends to fill the other vacant spots. Oh sure, I could've chosen random people that I knew, but that seemed odd to me. Mike, on the other hand, had two guys from his department, plus Gabe.

I like the orange pekoe, too, Lucifuge whispered. I could almost feel him behind me, appraising how he might take me over.

My heart dropped into my stomach. *Not now, Lucifuge.*

I have a serious question though, the Daemon countered. *I need to know how your astral magick skills are.*

I fiddled with the handle of my cup. *Lucifuge, this is a really bad time.*

Your astral magick skills, he persisted.

They're fine, I guess, I thought.

Fine? Lucifuge sounded concerned. *We're going to have to work on that.*

I shoved my mind forward - focusing on the conversation at the table.

"We'll simply have Mike's sister and niece stand in," Beverly said. She ran an aging, thin hand through her currently short salt-and-pepper hair. She usually dyed it blonde, but the dye was growing out. That seems strange for Beverly, since appearances were everything. "After all, we can't have too many groomsmen and not enough bridesmaids. It will look ridiculous."

With a stifled yawn, Mike nodded. "That makes sense, unless Liz would like to have her cousin stand in for her."

I wasn't about to tell them that I would not wish wedding chore duties on my poor unsuspecting cousin, who was currently only four months pregnant, but by the time the wedding happened, her belly would be full with child. Instead, I shrugged. "We can have Mike's sister and niece stand in. I'm fine with that."

Kenny DeBeers emptied his teacup and leaned back. "Now we just need to choose the cake, and we can work out other details as we go. Unless you have ideas about the color of the tablecloths."

Beverly raised an eyebrow and pulled back slightly. "White, obviously."

I wanted to make a remark something like, *isn't white only reserved for virgins?* But I held my tongue. There was no sense in starting a fight. Besides, I was just beginning to feel like Beverly actually liked me - in her own strange way. I knew it was a lot better than her not liking me, and if possible, I wanted our relationship to continue to improve. If for no other reason than to keep the family peace.

When was the last time you did astral magick, Lucifuge chimed in.

He wasn't going to leave me alone unless I answered. *I don't remember. A while?*

Oh dear. Then I felt the Daemon retreat.

Beverly rose and began collecting cups from the table. "Go change, dear. We'll go to the cake shop and look at cakes."

I looked at Mike and he looked at me. That seemed rather sudden. Earlier she had said we *might* go.

"You too, Michael," she said.

I don't know if Mike thought he could get out of it, but he looked down at himself and said, "I look fine. I'm sure people in jeans and T-shirts shop for cake all the time."

His mother rolled her eyes and gave me an exasperated look. "Men."

I felt the corners of my mouth upturn into a grin, and I nodded and stood before making my way out of the kitchen without looking back. I would probably get in trouble for that smirk later. Or at least teased for it. Mike had to know I'd only given the nod because it was his mother and more than anything it was about keeping the peace.

I slipped upstairs to change into a pair of jeans and a blue blouse. Mike snuck into the bedroom as I was putting on my shoes.

"Do I have to go to this?"

"It's just cake. This is the easiest thing you'll have to do. I promise," I said, my voice trailing off and my gaze fixating at the wall. Why did the Daemon want to know about astral magick?

"Liz?"

I drew my attention back to Mike and shook my head. "Lucifuge asked me earlier how long it's been since I did astral magick and if I was any good at it."

"Why?" Mike frowned.

I shrugged. "Don't know. But it's bugging me. I mean, does he want to me do astral magick? If so – what?"

"Maybe after we get back from testing cake, you can ask him, but right now, we need to get this cake thing done and over with." Mike took off his t-shirt and put on a pale blue, button-down shirt. It was clear he wasn't going to change anything else he was wearing.

"You're right. I need to focus on wedding stuff."

"Are you sure you don't want to ask your cousin instead of my sister and niece?"

"I can ask, but she's pregnant and she may not even be up to coming to the wedding. We'll see. I'll throw the offer out there, and we'll figure it out." I started toward the door, trying to focus, but in the back of my mind, all I could worry about was astral magick.

Thirty minutes later, we found ourselves in a small strip mall cake shop, sitting in plastic chairs around a plastic table. It was a lot less posh than I expected. In my mind, Beverly only shopped at large stores or shops, with servants and handmaidens. Or something like that. Mike and I sat together across from Beverly and Kenny. In front of each of us on the table were laminated lists of cake flavors. I liked cake as much as the next person, but this was ridiculous. A young woman, about twenty-five, her sable hair pulled back into a ragged ponytail, approached the table, chafing her hands against her flour-dusted apron. "Do you know which flavors you'd like to try?"

This time, Beverly seemed as baffled by the sheer number of flavors as we were. She looked across the table at Mike and I, helpless, and said nothing.

Mike also deferred to me and said nothing. So, with a shrug, I said, "Let's do German chocolate, dark chocolate, raspberry chocolate, yellow, Bavarian cream, and red velvet." I figured that was plenty of flavors. White cakes were always too dry, and really, how many flavors of chocolate did you actually need?

Kenny DeBeers reached over and took me and Mike's laminated cake menu, setting it next to him and Beverly's as if to compare them to see if there were any discrepancies. He said nothing. The young baker disappeared into the back with our list of flavors. While we waited, we sat looking at each other uncomfortably, as if conversation was something foreign. It's not like we didn't have anything to talk about. After all, we were planning Beverly's dream wedding. Or rather the wedding she dreamed of for her son. In that moment, I did find myself a little irritated, but I decided not to dwell on the feeling.

You were going to have cake without me. Lucifuge's smooth voice whispered through my mind like a hiss.

You can't be here right now, I scolded him inwardly. *My mother-in-law's here and we're in a public space. If you're going to turn my eyes red and start making snarky comments...* I hated being so upfront with the Daemon, but I didn't want him thinking it was okay to do whatever he wanted in my body. If he was going to possess me, it would be on my terms. I was just setting boundaries. Surely, he would understand.

Of course, I understand, Lucifuge said. *But if I recall I was promised cake. I promise not to turn your eyes red.*

I narrowed my eyes. I had an idea. *Fine, you can try one bite of each flavor on several conditions…*

Okay, Lucifuge sounded cautious. As well he should have.

First, I have to be able to taste each flavor too because I'm the one who has to choose the cake. Second, there will be no Daemonic commentary. If my mother-in-law realizes I'm possessed, she's going to have a fit and she'll call all of the witchy exorcists she can find to chase you off. Third, you have to tell me why you were asking about astral magick.

There was a long pause before Lucifuge finally said, *All right.*

I felt Mike touch my arm and pulled my attention from within myself to everyone at the table. I noticed Beverly and Kenny DeBeers giving me a funny look. "Oh, sorry. I just thinking about something work-related," I lied.

"It must've been something that really pissed you off. You look like you were going to kill someone," Mike said.

Beverly's eyes went wide. "Michael. Watch your tongue. I won't have you engaging in gutter speak when we're in public." She shot Kenny DeBeers an apologetic look.

Kenny fiddled with his hands in his lap and gave her a slight nod. "It's quite alright. I've heard worse."

"Hopefully not from anyone in my family," Beverly mumbled. Her eyes darted to the door that led into the back where all the ovens must've been. "How long could possibly take to cut several pieces of cake?"

"Have some patience, mom. I'm sure we're not their only customers." Mike leaned on the table with his elbows and shook his head.

"I wasn't expecting this to take hours of time. Merely a half hour," she said, brushing it off as if she wasn't nearly as snooty as everyone thought she was.

I stifled a giggle.

I think she's right, Lucifuge said in my mind. *It can't possibly take someone that long to get a few pieces of cake. Where do they have to go to get it? The seventh sphere?*

Lucifuge appeared to have a wry sense of humor. It certainly didn't bother me, but I did wonder if perhaps the Daemon appeared to me that way because he knew that was the way in which I'd be most receptive to what he had to say. Not to mention his proposition of using my body to infiltrate some type of doomsday cult. An alleged Satanic doomsday cult, no less.

One set on bringing about Armageddon, he clarified.

With astral magick? Never mind, we'll talk about this later, I thought. *Right now, we are here for cake and nothing else.*

The Daemon gave me a mental nod and said nothing.

Just as Kenny DeBeers had begun talking about the weather in a forced attempt at small talk, the young woman appeared with a large platter filled with small plates and tiny pieces of cake. No wonder it had taken her so long. On each paper plate was written the flavor, and each plate contained four small pieces of cake, two bites each. I couldn't help but think it was a good thing they had given us larger pieces, so that I could share the cake eating experience with Lucifuge.

My mouth began to water as if I'd been anticipating cake for months. It had to be the Daemon and not me. I knew what cake tasted like and didn't require a refresher. Then again, in all fairness, I hadn't tasted this cake. Beverly insisted it was some of the best cake along the front range. Who was I to argue?

Our bakery hostess set the large platter down onto the table and produced four white plastic forks, handing one to each of us. "If you'd like to try other flavors, or you need additional pieces of these, please let me know. I'll just be in the back there." Then she turned on her heel and disappeared back through the door behind the counter.

Lucifuge jumped into my body. It was like a jolt that seemed to suck the air from my lungs. Once he was settled perfectly, he drew in a deep breath and rubbed his hands together, or rather my hands, in perfect anticipation.

I could still see out of my eyes. Mike gave me an odd sideways glance then reached out and put his arm over the platter and said, "Let's each take one plate and distribute flavors onto everyone's plate, if that makes sense."

Beverly furrowed her brow, which she did a lot, and said, "Not articulated very well, but I think we all understood what you mean." Then together, she and Mike began distributing the various flavors of cake to where each of us only had one plate with each of the selections on it.

"Well, that was genius, because now we don't know what flavor is what. Hopefully, we can figure it out," I heard my own voice say. The Daemon shook my head.

Don't get salty, I told him.

Lucifuge laughed. "I think I'll make my way through the chocolate first," he said.

Mike shot me another weird look. A look that said, *what the hell has gotten into you?* I guessed that he would have it figured out soon enough. Mike and I were close, he would undoubtedly notice the shift in personality, and then come to the horrific realization that it was currently Lucifuge trying wedding cake and not me.

Lucifuge had no intention of allowing me to come forward. He did, however, make it to where I could taste the cake as well. He wanted to taste along with me, both bites, not just one for him and one for me. I was fine with that because while he was stuffing my craw with cake, he wasn't talking or raising suspicion with Beverly and Kenny. Mike, on the other hand, kept giving me strange looks, so I knew he had probably picked up on it.

Not surprisingly, my plate was cleared before anyone else's. Lucifuge sat back in the chair, his gaze on the now empty plate.

"You want more?" Mike asked, his voice laden with both amusement and sarcasm. *Amarcasm*, I thought with an inward titter.

"Only if you're not going to eat it," the Daemon said. "I think the German chocolate and the red velvet cake are my favorites. But for the more boring guests, you should probably do a tier of the yellow cake too." The Daemon took the cake Mike offered him, taking huge bites and letting the cake melt in my mouth and linger at the back of my tongue before swallowing. "People just don't realize what a treat this is," Lucifuge told Mike. "The physical act of eating something is such a wondrous thing. The taste, the texture. It's exquisite. I can see why so many people eat to excess and die from such maladies."

Stuck in the back of my mind, it was like watching a movie. Not a very good one. Both Beverly and Kenny DeBeers were giving me strange looks, as if I had sprouted two heads. I wondered then if Lucifuge had turned my eyes red. Mike, however, gave no knowing indication that anything was off. But I knew better, he was just trying to play like everything was normal as to not arouse suspicion. By the look on Beverly's face, I could tell there was probably a private discussion about this coming, once Kenny DeBeers was out of the picture.

Lucifuge finished all of the uneaten cake on the table and, once he was done, he jumped out of my body as quickly as he jumped in. As he left, I felt like a plug had been pulled and my blood was draining away. Lightheaded dizziness overcame me, and I grabbed at the table for support.

"Well, you shouldn't have eaten that much cake. Now you're sick," Beverly said in a scolding tone. She shook her head and gave Mike a look. A look I knew meant they would be having a private conversation about my behavior later on, and I probably wouldn't be involved in it. Or if I was, I was going to be scolded and told to behave better the next time. Perhaps she'd send me to some type of debutante coach to teach me how to be a proper lady. I groaned inwardly. To be honest, that sounded like something Beverly would do.

Instead of arguing, I just nodded. "Sorry about that. I just really like cake," I said, looking down at my hands, trying to appear ashamed of myself.

Mike stifled a snicker and reached down to my lap to take one of my hands into his. "So, we're going with one tier of the German chocolate, one tier of the red velvet cake, and one tier of the yellow, right?"

Lucifuge did have good taste in cake because, quite frankly, I agreed with his choices. I nodded. "Yeah, let's go with that. What did you think, Beverly?"

I expected nothing less than contrary from Beverly, and she didn't disappoint. "I quite preferred the dark chocolate, but those three weren't bad. I suppose they'll do. Those flavors are a bit *common*, but it is *your* wedding." She beamed a forced smile at us from across the table.

After we decided on the shape of the cake and the flavors, Kenny DeBeers told the baker what we wanted, but told her that he would have to call in the size since we were still waiting on a headcount for how many people we needed to feed.

As we were leaving, us getting into Mike's Jeep and Beverly and Kenny getting into Beverly's Mercedes, Beverly said, "I'll call you tonight, Michael. Don't forget the next weekend we're going to the caterers to try the various dishes for the wedding reception." That was it. No goodbye, no go fuck yourself, not even a glare or stern look at me as she left.

Once we were alone in the safety of the Jeep, I turned to Mike. "Thanks for covering for me back there. I'm sorry you're going to have to have a conversation with your mother later about me and my behavior."

Mike laughed. "She really doesn't hate you like you think she does. She was just raised a certain way and can't deal with anything outside her own normal. You know that."

"Just whatever you do, don't tell her that I'm possessed by a damn Daemon."

Mike turned the ignition and carefully backed out of the parking space. "I don't know, maybe I should tell her you were possessed by a Daemon so that way I can save myself a half hour of her bitching about how you much you embarrassed her in front of Kenny DeBeers."

I groaned and realized that, at that very moment, I would have much rather been brushing up on my astral magick. That was far less complicated.

Great, Lucifuge said. *We'll start tonight.*

CHAPTER 5

et up, we need to act today, Lucifuge said. A vision of a horned god, with weathered skin and glowing red eyes, leaned into me and with one taloned finger, tapped me right in the middle of my forehead. I bolted upright in bed, my heart racing in my chest. I gasped for air and could still feel a buzzing where the talon had pressed into my skin. Mike sat up next to me.

He leaned toward me and took my arm in his hand. "Are you okay? Bad dream?"

In the still dark bedroom, I couldn't see his face, but I could feel the concern in his touch. "Bad dream," I said, not really wanting to say anything else about it. I turned my eyes to the window, noticing it was still pitch-black outside. My gaze fell to the bedside clock, its angry red digital display declaring it was four o'clock in the morning. I groaned and threw myself back onto my pillow, pressing my palms into my eyes. It was too early to get up and my body ached from the lack of sleep from the night before. It hadn't helped that before bed I'd spent several hours practicing astral magick with Lucifuge. Let's just say the Daemon had a way of making me feel inadequate.

My mind replayed the training session: Lucifuge and I in my celestial temple. He, a lone shadow figure standing in the corner, watched as I did a basic elemental balancing ritual.

"No, no, no," Lucifuge had said after the first performance.

"I'm doing the ritual right," I complained. With an exasperated huff, I slumped.

"You're just going through the motions. You need to *see* and *feel* the colors. You need to *see* and *feel* the invocations. They need to *vibrate* at the core of your very being," he said in a stern voice. "Do it again."

That had been the entire session over and over with recurring and new criticisms each time, for hours.

I glanced at the clock again, then literally shook my head as if that would wipe my memory of the astral session and the subsequent dream. Then I drew in a deep breath and yawned.

"Try to go back to sleep. Get a few more hours," Mike whispered. Then he settled back into his own pillow and drew the blankets up over his shoulders.

I took another cleansing breath, closed my eyes, and tried to relax, but it was no use. My mind raced. The dream image of the Daemon had been jarring. I much preferred them as shadows, figures in the corner of my eye, like Lucifuge had been in the temple the night before. Outright physical manifestation, even if it was only a dream, could still shake a person to the core. Even so, adrenalin couldn't last forever. With a yawn, I felt my heart slow and my mind begin drifting back into the deep depths of a dark dreamscape.

Yet, I didn't remember any dreams after that. I also didn't remember Mike slipping out of bed because he was careful not to wake me, not even when he drew the curtains to keep the sunlight out. It wasn't until noon the next day that I felt him sit on the edge of the bed next to me and gently shake me by the shoulder. "Hey, are you going to get up?"

I groaned, grabbed my pillow, and put it over my head. "No."

"Are you sure? There might be cake downstairs." Then he snickered.

"That's not funny," I said into the pillow.

Mike laughed. "I know, but I know you'd be angry with me if I let you sleep all day. Do you have anything you have to do for work?"

"Nope." I left the pillow over my head to block out what little light seeped into the room from around the drawn black curtains. We'd hung dark curtains in the bedroom to block out as much light as possible since sometimes Mike worked odd hours and needed to sleep during the day.

"Well, I'm not going to make you get up, then. But don't be mad at me if you sleep your Sunday away. Oh, and I talked to my mom. You should know that she didn't say a damn word about you, which surprised me too," he said, standing. I heard his footfalls near the door.

"What did she say?" My curiosity got the best of me. I found Beverly's lack of commentary disturbing.

"She wanted to tell me that an uncle I've only met a handful of times is coming to the wedding. It seems it's a big deal. Something to do with coven gifts or something. She appeared to think it was pretty important, but I don't know him that well, so I guess it just isn't that big of a deal to me. Not like it is to her. So, naturally, I humored her and acted surprised and excited because I'm pretty sure that's how she wanted me to react." I imagined him shrugging his shoulders like he usually did.

I pulled the pillow off of my head and looked at him, his silhouette framed by the light filtering in through the bedroom door. "Maybe I'll get up in a few minutes. Can we just order in for lunch slash dinner? I don't feel like cooking."

Mike nodded. "Sure. Pizza, sandwiches, or Chinese?"

That was pretty much all you could get delivered in this town unless you wanted to call one of those new delivery services that charged ten dollars or more to pick up food from your favorite restaurant. "Chinese. I want Mushu beef."

"All right. I'll order it in about an hour unless you're hungry now?" He lingered in the doorway for a moment.

"An hour is fine," I said. I had every intention of trying to fall back to sleep, even if it was only for the next half hour. "I'll be down in a few minutes."

"Uh huh," Mike said as he closed the door behind him.

I closed my eyes and felt my head grow heavy on the pillow behind me and I groaned again. "Lucifuge," I said beneath my breath, "Can this wait for at least another day or two?"

What was supposed to be a joyous time in my life was turning out to be an outright pain in the ass.

The next thing I remember was the distant sound of the doorbell from far below. It sounded like it was ringing from the abyss. With a whimper, I forced myself into a sitting position and tried to shake off the grogginess. I looked at the clock; it was already four in the afternoon. I didn't bother changing out of my pajamas or putting on slippers. I was wearing socks, and so I padded across the bedroom to the door and opened it, leaning out into the hallway so I could hear who it was. Nothing. I heard the low muffle of the television from the living room. It sounded like Mike was watching one of those reality shows where people figured out the worth of all their old junk.

I stepped into the hallway and leaned over the railing to the rooms below. "Mike?"

"Yeah, babe," came his voice from the dining room.

"Is that dinner?"

"Dinner's in the fridge. You up?" He came around to the foyer so I could see him.

"Yeah. I'll be down in a few minutes." I almost laughed at myself because I was pretty sure I told him that at least twice earlier in the day. This time, however, I meant it. I took a few minutes in the bathroom and ten minutes later found myself walking down the stairs debating whether or not my stomach could really handle Chinese food. For some reason, I just wasn't that hungry. Perhaps it had been the cake from the day before. No, I quickly decided. It had to be stress. The wedding was drawing nearer, work was made more of a challenge with my former incompetent secretary, and Lucifuge was so damn random. The Daemon had me so on edge that I was even having dreams about him and his secret mission.

As I reached the bottom of the stairs, Lucifuge pressed into my thoughts. *Okay, pay attention. You need to listen carefully, or we won't be able to stop this*, the Daemon said.

Again? I thought, *Can't this wait another day or two?*

I think that's out of our hands now. You've just been recruited. Then Lucifuge went silent.

I knew exactly what he meant the second I stepped into the dining room. Mike was sitting there sifting through several folders.

He held his palms pressed together, his fingers at his lips, staring intently into the contents of the file splayed open before him.

"How long has the food been here?" I asked, sauntering over to the fridge and opening it only to find the large brown bag filled with Chinese food not yet opened.

"Couple hours," he said, not really looking at me. "Before you pull out the food, look at this." He dropped his hands to the table and began sifting through the folders again.

I sat at my normal spot and folded my hands in front of me on the table. Mike pushed a folder to me, and I pulled my hands back. The picture staring back at me was that of a dark-haired man with equally dark eyes, in his late thirties. Thirty-eight to be exact, according to the birthdate next to his name. I couldn't help but stare at those eyes. Eyes that belonged to Benjamin Stone, alias Drakaris Deathspell. I turned that page over and began shuffling through the remainder of the file. The man had a long list of traffic violations and an arrest record that included domestic violence, forgery, identity theft, and petty thievery. "What's this?"

"Our next case." He gave me a look that said *I hate to do this to you, but…* "It's the cult Lucifuge told us about."

"The FBI wants us? Both of us?" I don't even know why I asked when I already knew the answer. The only reason Mike and I were pulled into a case as a team was if it was somehow occult related. I really wished I'd known what was up with all the strange occult cases we been getting in the last year. While Denver did have a large occult community, and the city was growing now that cannabis was legal, we hadn't had this much negative activity, ever. Not that I knew of, anyway.

"One of my friends in the local FBI dropped this off. They've been watching this guy because they heard he's been planning to plant bombs in stadiums and large venues in Denver, Topeka, Phoenix, and a few other places. All throughout the west here. Even Vegas. They've been monitoring his social media, too. He's a self-proclaimed Satanic priest." Mike lifted an eyebrow. "I guess Lucifuge was right."

"Was there ever any doubt?"

"I guess not," Mike conceded.

"Everybody thinks they are a Satanic priest these days. That doesn't make it so." I snorted at the thought. It was true. Nowadays in the occult community, everybody and their mother was a priest. Very few of them really understood what it was to hold such a position. Most of the time they just wanted followers, respect, and power because they didn't have those things in their day-to-day life.

Mike didn't respond to my snarky comment. "He runs this group called the Antichrist's Temple. According to sources, they believe they are doing the devil's work on earth and bringing about Armageddon."

Uttering the word *Armageddon* was all it took for Lucifuge to jump into my body. He immediately took over. "I was right, wasn't I? Now you see why I need Elizabeth."

Mike let out a disgruntled sigh and motioned to the folder. "It seems so. My FBI friend said he might need our help, but there was no mention of sending you and Elizabeth in. I don't think I could talk them into that. They're just interested in her insight or any connections Liz might have to get us closer to this guy." He tipped his head to one side and gave the Daemon a thoughtful look. "She's in there right now? She can hear me?"

I was, and I could. "Yes," Lucifuge said. He proceeded to thumb through the file, barely glancing at any of the information. The Daemon already knew most of it. "Well, tell them that Elizabeth will wear a wire and she could easily make them trust her. She could get the information that we need, and the FBI, Homeland security, or whoever can come in and arrest them all and take them away for all I care. I just need to stop them because the lives of thousands are at stake."

The Daemon knew more than he was saying. His energy withdrew when he hesitated. I wasn't in a position to really question him, *yet*, so I just sat back and listened.

Mike's piercing gaze caught me for a moment and then he looked away toward the fridge. "Would you like some Chinese food, Lucifuge? Have you ever had Chinese?"

I felt my eyes widen as Lucifuge's interest grew. "I have not. What is it, exactly?"

As Mike and Lucifuge discussed the merits and sauces of Chinese food, I thought about Benjamin Stone, alias Ben Stone and Drakaris Deathspell, and what mental malady a man must have to create bombs meant to kill thousands of people. Getting that close to someone that crazy wasn't something I was looking forward to doing. Especially with explosives involved. People didn't walk away from C-4. Then I thought of suicide bombers and, again, for the life of me, I couldn't imagine the mental state it would take to want to take one's own life and destroy it. All for some strange religious belief that dying for a cause was righteous and holy. I couldn't imagine wanting to be a martyr for anything. In that moment the gravity of the situation hit me like a brick in the chest and my job, the wedding, family, friends - it all seemed terribly petty.

Mike and Lucifuge set the folders aside and dug into microwaved Chinese food as I sat back in the recesses of my mind while the Daemon stuffed my face with fried rice and sweet and sour chicken. At least I wasn't going to starve while possessed. It almost seemed as though Mike and Lucifuge were getting a bit chummy, which I didn't mind since Mike was forever the skeptic - or perhaps not after this. At least he'd now have the experience of having communicated with a Daemon, so maybe he could better understand me when I talked about spirit communication.

While they ate, I thought about Drakaris Deathspell – gods, such a stupid name - and why Lucifuge would be so interested in taking this guy out. Thousands of people died daily due to terrorism and other atrocities. So why did the Daemon insist on us infiltrating the cult? Was it just because they were doing this in Satan's name? No, I quickly decided, it couldn't be that. People did stupid things in the name of the Christian devil all the time. There was something bigger going on here, but for the life of me, I couldn't imagine what it was.

The guys, if Lucifuge counted as a guy, finished eating and for the third time that day, our doorbell rang.

"I should go. Thank you for the Chinese food. We'll talk later," Lucifuge said casually.

Mike nodded in acknowledgment and got up to go answer the door, leaving me to the woozy sensation of coming back into my body.

By the time I'd come to, Alyssa and Gabe strode into the large kitchen-dining room with Mike leading them. Mike hurried to the table, leaned across it, and scooped up the files, putting them back into the brown expandable file folder they'd come in. Then he took it over to the *shit collector* and dropped it there with a thump.

"So how are you guys?" Mike asked.

"We thought we'd stop by to say hi and to see if you wanted to go get a bite to eat," Gabe said.

"We just had Chinese," I said, jumping in. I could still taste the sweet pineapple on my lips. "There's a ton left over if you guys want some."

"We could do that," Alyssa said, looking to Gabe for agreement. She tossed her purse on the table and started toward the kitchen on her own. That's the kind of friends we were. She didn't ask to rummage through my kitchen for food or drink, and I didn't expect her to. She also didn't have to ask where anything was, because she knew. She and Gabe had helped us move and unpack.

Mike gave me an odd look as if gauging whether or not it was me, then stepped up behind me and gave my shoulders a warm squeeze. "So, did you see the game yesterday?"

It was obviously directed at Gabe, who nodded while dumping a generous spoonful of fried rice on his plate. "Yeah. The Steelers aren't playing well."

Mike snorted. "You're not a Broncos fan?"

"Only when they're not playing a team I like better," he said, snickering.

That's when I realized I had forgotten to leave out my offerings of wine and incense for the day and that was much preferable to listening to sports talk. Mike wasn't much of a sports guy, but when a friend of his liked sports, he faked it well. "I have to go tend the altar," I said, standing suddenly. "Totally forgot to leave my offerings today."

The room went quiet and Alyssa gently set her plate on the counter. "I'll warm this up in a few. Keep the cat out of it. I'll help Liz with the offerings."

Together, we went upstairs to the spare bedroom that served as our temple. It would have been a dedicated temple space, but with the wedding looming, I needed all the space I could get to keep family and friends from having to rent hotel rooms.

"So how are things going with your little possession problem?" Alyssa asked, closing the door of the temple behind us. I set about grabbing a charcoal from the drawer of my altar.

I split the black disk out of the foil packet and plunked it down into the cast iron cauldron. From the same drawer, I pulled out a bag of white copal. "He only seems to come around when it's time to eat, and if I didn't know any better, I'd think Lucifuge and Mike are becoming friends, which is weird."

She laughed. "He's not showing up when you guys are, uh, getting busy?"

Biting back laughter, I shook my head at the mortifying thought. "Gods no! But he showed up during cake testing with Mike's mom. At least he didn't pull the red-eye bit. The wedding planner was there, too. That would have been disastrous." I took up the long lighter and ignited the charcoal, then gave her shrug.

Alyssa crossed her arms over her chest and her mood turned sober. "What is that he wants you to do exactly?"

I shrugged again. "He thinks that I am going to thwart some doomsday cult. With his help of course. For some reason, he keeps insisting I do astral meditations to perform banal rituals. Like elemental balancing and self-purification."

"Hmm. That's interesting."

"Why?" I cocked my head to one side, curious.

"It just seems rather specific." She poked at one of the oil lamps on the altar. "So how are you supposed to thwart a doomsday cult with astral meditation and ritual?"

I hadn't given it much thought and found myself stumped by the question. "The thing is, the FBI is already investigating the cult. I don't see why they just can't send someone from the FBI in undercover. Clearly, they need someone in the know when it comes to explosives because that's what the FBI suspects these people of doing: making bombs."

"Maybe he expects you to defeat them with astral ritual in some way," she suggested. "How did the FBI find them, anyway?"

"Their manifesto was leaked, and they were targeting large venues like football stadiums and concert halls. You know, take out as many as you can. Although I don't know if it was a suicide bomber thing or if they plan to just place the bombs, run away, and ignite them with a remote. That's not my department."

Alyssa watched me drop a few large pieces of the copal resin onto the charcoal, and a thick white smoke began to rise from the cauldron. I drew in a deep breath and almost coughed. It was easy to forget how pungent copal could be. From beneath the altar, I pulled out a flask of wine, uncorked it, and poured a small amount into the chalice on the altar. Then I lit the altar candle.

She wrinkled her nose at the copal. "The astral stuff doesn't make sense then. Especially if this is a real world, physical problem."

I shrugged. "Maybe he just wants me to be mentally strong, especially if he gets his way and I end up getting close to the leader." I had an idea then. I paused and lifted a finger. "Maybe the cult brainwashes people and all this astral work is meant to keep me from being susceptible."

"Ah." She nodded as if that made perfect sense. "That sounds plausible," she said, her eyes now on the smoke lifting from the cauldron.

"So how are you and Gabe doing," I asked, eager to change the subject. I never asked Alyssa about her job because she always told me it was the same thing, different day. I never asked about Gabe's job because she would always groan and roll her eyes.

Alyssa tipped her head to one side. "Everything's good."

Alyssa and Gabe had been together longer than me and Mike, so I'd occasionally wondered if they would end up getting married as well. They never talked about it, and I didn't ask. I figured that was none of my business, plus I didn't want to sound like one of those annoying women who constantly asked their unmarried friends when they were going to get married. Honestly, before I met Mike, I never imagined myself the marrying type.

"Good, that's it? I haven't seen you guys in a couple of weeks, minus the other night with the whole Daemon possession incident but, something interesting must be going on in your lives."

Alyssa laughed, but it was fake. Her facial expression turned to concern instead of amusement, and she withdrew into herself slightly.

"What..." That's when I felt the surge of the Daemon entering my body through my head, spreading out down into my limbs and torso. Once again, my consciousness was shoved into the back of my head, and while I could still see and hear, I no longer had control of my limbs or my mouth. "She is your best friend. You should tell her."

Alyssa visibly gulped and gave me an incredulous look. "Lucifuge?"

"Who else? I'm the only Daemon claiming Elizabeth for my use. So why are you lying? One of the joys of being a physical creature is being able to reproduce. Are you not happy about this?" Lucifuge wrinkled my nose at the scent of the copal and turned to look at the altar. "That's never been my favorite scent."

I found myself stunned, not even wanting to address the Daemon's comment about copal. Alyssa was pregnant and she hadn't told me? The feeling of shock subsided into feelings of disappointment and betrayal. How could my best friend leave me out of the loop on something so important? It was a huge revelation.

"Elizabeth's feelings are hurt that you didn't tell her," Lucifuge told her without my permission.

Alyssa's eyes traveled to her feet and she started fidgeting with her hands. "I wasn't sure yet and I didn't want to steal Liz and Mike's thunder, okay? They're getting married. I'm going to be pregnant for several months after their wedding." With a chagrined look she shrugged at the Daemon, adding, "Once I found out for sure – of course I was going to tell her. But if you're telling me now, then I guess I'll be getting a phone call from the doctor's office telling me the blood test came back positive, won't I?"

"I could tell you the sex of it if you want," Lucifuge said. He made my voice sound cold and uncaring, but because I was connected to the Daemon, I could tell that he was just trying to be helpful.

Alyssa lifted a finger at the Daemon in my body and said, "Don't you dare. I don't want to know."

"But don't you want to know the types of things you should probably buy?" Lucifuge seemed confused. "You separate gender by garment color, right?"

Alyssa took a step toward me, her fingers still pointed at the Daemon. "If you do – I'm going to exorcise you right now."

Alyssa, I scolded inwardly. We didn't command Daemons in this house. We worked with them. However, there had been a few times I've been forceful with Lucifuge, but only because he was squatting in my body, and I had a right to some boundaries. Threatening to exorcise him, however, had never really been on my agenda. Mike's perhaps, but not mine. And the only reason Mike would've done such a thing, or attempted it, was because he was worried about me. He wouldn't have thought of it otherwise

"Very well. I was just trying to be helpful." The Daemon reached out and picked up the chalice on my altar, brought it to my nose and took a deep whiff. "That smells good." He brought the chalice to his lips and took a small taste of the wine, then scrunched my nose and put it back. He looked at Alyssa and shook my head. "It doesn't taste as good as it smells."

Alyssa snickered, her face finally relaxing and her arms retreating to her sides. "You didn't need to jump into Elizabeth while she was talking to me. Can I have her back now please?"

"Of course," Lucifuge said. Just like that he pulled out through the top of my head and I felt momentarily dizzy, reaching out and grabbing onto the altar for support.

"Liz?" Alyssa stepped toward me with her hands at my elbow to steady me.

"Yeah, I'm good," I told her. "He does that sometimes. Usually when he thinks he has something to say or do. It's usually food that brings him out. Maybe it was the wine or the copal," I mused.

Alyssa let out a deep, forlorn sigh. "I'm sorry I didn't say anything, it's just that you have so much going on, the last thing you needed was me worrying about whether or not I'm pregnant and all that," she said.

I had momentarily forgotten that I was upset with her about that, but it made sense. She wouldn't want to tell us anything if the test came back negative. Clearly, however, the test would be positive. I was kind of disappointed she didn't take Lucifuge up on the offer to know the sex of the baby. It would've made baby shower shopping and planning so much easier. But I didn't tell her that. "I'm really excited for you guys. How is Gabe taking the news?"

"I haven't really said anything to him either." She withdrew slightly and cringed, then lowered her voice. "I don't know if he's going to like this much at all. He doesn't like kids. I didn't mean for this to happen. I'm on birth control, even. Though in retrospect I sometimes miss a dose here and there."

"Well, did you ever talk about what you would do if it did happen? I mean, being a Satanist and all, you think you two would talk about the spirituality you would bring your children up with. Or if you'd do rituals in front of them. These are things couples talk about, aren't they?" These were things Mike and I had talked about extensively. Mike didn't want his kids growing up completely ignorant of what we practiced like his own mother had done to him. While he did agree that it was good to allow children to find their own way spiritually, he'd also been pretty upset to discover that his mother had been lying to him for well over thirty years.

"We don't really talk about things like that. We did once talk about getting a marriage license if we ever decided to buy a house together, but strictly for insurance and legal reasons. Like wills and health care and stuff. I don't think I'm the kind of girl who gets married." There was a tinge of fear in her eyes. "I don't really think I'm mother material either. Oh my gods, Liz! What if I'm a terrible mother?"

I reached out and took her hand into mine and patted it gently, giving her a reassuring smile. "You would be the coolest mom ever. Besides, we all have to grow up sometime. You and Gabe included. If I have to get married by Beverly's decree and endure all the flowers and cakes and whatever else she has planned, perhaps it's time that you and Gabe think about settling down, buying a house, getting married and raising that baby."

That incredulous look crossed her face again. "Just because I'm having a kid doesn't mean I have to settle down." Her face fell. "Does it?"

I gave her a half-hearted smile and a nod. "It might."

"Oh gods, we're getting old." Her face contorted into a pout.

"Well, we all have problems," I said. Then I laughed. "We're not getting any younger, and you're no longer the carefree Satanic cheerleader you were when you were a teenager, even though I didn't really know you back then, but I've heard the stories. If I'm settling down into married life, I have room in my life for friends with children."

"I really don't know how I'm going to tell Gabe. I was really hoping I wasn't. But all the stick tests confirmed that I was." She let out a sigh.

"Well, I think you should wait for sure for confirmation from the doctor, and I'd leave Lucifuge's confirmation out of the conversation. That way you can sit down and say, hey look, I'm pregnant. We're going to have a kid, what names do you like?" I tossed my hands up like it was no big deal and was happy when the gesture made Alyssa laugh.

"You do realize I'm not going to fit in a damn bridesmaid's dress, right?" She sighed again. "Goodbye, firm and trim body."

Laughter tumbled from the back of my throat, and I couldn't stop laughing. The only thing that brought me out of my fit of giggles was a knock on the door. "What you two doing in there?" It was Mike. "Let Alyssa come down and eat."

"Nothing, girl talk." Then I sat and waited for a response. None came, so I assumed Mike was either listening at the door or had gone back downstairs. "I suppose we should get back down before they're both outside the door. Don't worry, your secret is safe with me, but you're going to have to tell him the second you find out. And don't worry about the stupid bridesmaid dress. I'll look for a style that can accommodate a woman with child."

Alyssa cringed when I said that and shook her head. "I'll wear whatever you want me to, but yikes. Can you believe not five minutes ago I was talking to a Daemon as if it was nothing, and now we're talking about your wedding again?" She shook her head in disbelief and started out of the room.

I licked my thumb and forefinger and squeezed out the flame on the candle, a sign of respect to the fire element. Once I was satisfied that the candle flame was out, I made sure the trivet was firmly under the metal cauldron so it wouldn't burn the altar, and then I left the room with the door slightly ajar. That way if the altar caught on fire, I would smell it, at least.

The wedding, Alyssa becoming a mom, my new job. We were in our thirties now and had real responsibilities. It was time to get our shit together. In that moment I knew that it was also time for me to quit trying to pretend my life was normal and to step up and help the Daemon out. No one else was going to. I'd have to put my wedding plans on hold, or at least out of my mind since I was sure Beverly would have no issues continuing without me and take some time off of work.

CHAPTER 6

Normal people would have gone to the bridal shop to pick out dresses. My mother-in-law was not normal. No, I took off the afternoon from work, and she and Kenny DeBeers showed up with a woman whose name I didn't catch, and a large van. Inside the van were rolling garment racks filled with bridesmaids' dresses. I hadn't chosen the bridesmaids' dresses yet simply because I really wanted to get a feel for the entire wedding first, not to mention my own dress.

What are we looking for, the Daemon asked.

His voice was so subtle and unobtrusive that my mind reflexively answered. *I'm looking for something elegant. Something that will accommodate Alyssa's growing belly. She's going to be a few months in by the time she gets to wear the dress.*

The Daemon didn't say anything at first. I sensed his cool, detached observation. Finally, he said, *It's unfortunate it will be a dress she'll never wear again.*

Unless she has a cocktail party to attend while pregnant, I thought offhandedly.

Elegant, simple, and something that can be worn more than once, Lucifuge repeated, as if to make sure he understood me right.

Yes. Nothing is worse than having a dress in your closet that you can never wear again, I thought.

Two men removed the rolling racks from the truck and brought them straight in our front door, into the living room. Kenny, Beverly, and the strange woman who looked like she'd just walked off the pages of *Vogue* sat on the couch, scrutinizing the dresses. Occasionally, each of them passed me a look as if to see if I was paying attention. I was more concerned with Lucifuge's presence, and that I was underdressed for the occasion because I was only wearing a tank top and jeans.

Mike sat in a chair off to the side looking on warily. This wasn't his department, though it seemed he felt it would be rude if he left. Beverly would've taken it that way too.

"This seasons colors," the woman said to Beverly, then glanced at me as if she were trying to include me in a conversation that wasn't about me at all. She really knew who was running the show. "Are various shades of purple and blue. They're all the rage."

The phrase *all the rage* was about as outdated as my grandmother's douchebag. I didn't say anything. I wasn't sure I was a fan of purples at all. The only time I would have gone with purple was a deep purple, but in that case, I would've insisted that my wedding dress was black. I wasn't really the emo type, though a vampire-themed wedding would've probably been appropriate considering Mike's side of the guest list. My family would've been the odd ones out.

"Let's see what you have in blue," I said, squashing the idea of purple right then and there. I crossed my arms over my chest and gave the woman a forced smile. She stood and smoothed her dress with her long, skeletal fingers and put on that fake smile most people in retail wore when they were dealing with a difficult customer. One after another, she and her cadre of helpers pulled blue dresses from the racks. The blues they showed me were not blue. They were periwinkle and a dark blue with a purple tinge. The others were baby blue and turquoise. All of them, and the styles, were hideous.

I must've been frowning because Beverly said, "Perhaps we should look at swatches for colors. Let's concentrate on style."

I glanced over at Mike who was obviously fighting to keep a straight face, trying not to laugh. When he saw me looking, he bit his lower lip, scratched his neck, and said, "Does anyone want some tea or coffee or something?"

Everyone decided they wanted tea and for that Mike was grateful. He popped up out of the chair, practically tripping over his own feet in his eagerness to prepare it. He disappeared so quickly that I wasn't sure he was coming back. I didn't blame him. If I could have, I would have joined him. I had no doubt he would take his time, extending the chore as long as he possibly could so he didn't have to bear witness to this horrific ritual.

One by one the dresses were pulled from the rack and held out in front of all of us so we could examine the style. All of them were strapless except for the few that only had one strap over the left shoulder. Another had flared sleeves and looked like something a Mormon would wear.

You know, said Lucifuge, *they skipped one right there that they didn't pull out of that rack. They didn't show it to you. It's buried, right there. Do you see it?*

I groaned inwardly. *You shouldn't be here right now,* I thought. *This is a girl-dress thing, not a Daemon-Liz thing.*

Lucifuge ignored my attempt at setting boundaries. *If I can help you get through this faster, then I will. We have important work to do. You need more work in the astral. Your mind is strong, but a bit out of practice. All of this is just a distraction.*

Why do you keep wanting me to do astral work? For what reason? The thought of more sessions in the celestial temple made me bristle. I wasn't going to let him walk all over me. Then purposefully, I shoved him into the back of mind like an unwanted thought.

We can discuss that later.

Either you tell me now or you can get out, I thought, and set my jaw.

I see you're finally standing up for yourself, he said, amused.

Yeah, because you're crossing a line. Even in my mind, it sounded whiny.

You do realize one of the reasons I'm often called upon by magicians is to teach them to stand up for themselves and make decisions, the Daemon said.

Yeah, I wrote a book with you in it, I shot back sarcastically.

This time Lucifuge came at me, jumping straight into my frontal cortex. I could feel the force of his presence and it sent a buzz through my head. I tried to push back, but this time couldn't stop him. I hadn't yet mastered the art of blocking him completely. He was one of the stronger Daemons I'd encountered.

Then there was pressure on the top of my head, and I felt him slide into me, cool and ethereal. That familiar sensation flared in my neck, and a chill ran the length of my spine and through my arms. I gave into it. Perhaps I really didn't want the Daemon to leave. Though I was mortified at what he might do in front of Beverly and her guests.

With Lucifuge fully merged with me, I stood and briskly walked over to the rack of dresses, reached between two ugly periwinkle numbers that I'd already rejected, and pulled out the one hidden there. It was a deep shade of cobalt blue and had a halter neckline. It was ankle length and had plenty of room with the empire waist for a pregnant belly.

This one? Lucifuge asked inwardly.

Yes, I shouted in my head.

I felt Lucifuge glaring at the dress so intently I half expected it to go up in flames. *Now I just turn around and intimidate them,* he said.

No, I warned.

He turned. Out of my mouth, he said, "This one."

I pushed my mind forward to regain my faculties, forcing Lucifuge to the back.

Don't do that, Lucifuge said.

Then stop taking over, I said.

My stomach lurched and suddenly I had full control of my body. I threw the dress at the nearest person, and bolted past the shocked onlookers, through the living room, and up the stairs just as Mike entered with a tray of tea.

When I got to the top of the stairs, I stopped and pressed my back to the wall. Taking several deep, measured breaths, I closed my eyes.

"Michael," I heard Beverly say. "What is wrong with Elizabeth? She seems… preoccupied."

"She hasn't been feeling well," he lied without skipping a beat. Surely Beverly would see through such a flimsy lie, but he persisted. "She had an upset stomach earlier."

"Good gods, I hope she isn't pregnant," Beverly said. The clanking of cups followed, and I imagined Mike serving them their tea. I wondered what his expression said to Beverly at that moment.

"Mother, I assure you, she's not pregnant," Mike said.

"Good, because my guess is any wedding gown in a size eight is going to be a bit tight as it is. She might have to go up a size if she's not careful." Then Beverly paused. "That is a rather common shade of blue, but if that's what she wants. I guess the wedding colors are blue and white, and silver would match nicely with that. Don't you agree, Michael?"

"Yeah. You know, I'm going to go check on Liz," he said. Then I heard his footfalls approaching the steps.

I made no move to leave my position.

Then I heard Beverly say, "Make a note of this cobalt color."

Kenny DeBeers cleared his throat. "Noted."

Mike started up the stairs and stopped halfway up, noticing me standing there. He gave me his signature *what-the-fuck* look, and all I could manage was a weak smile. I couldn't do this today. No, there were far more important things to deal with, like helping Lucifuge so I could finally have some peace. When Mike reached the top of the stairs, he motioned to the bedroom, and I led the way. Once inside, he closed the bedroom door behind us, his face hard, practical. "What's going on?"

"It's too much," I blurted. I sat on the end of the bed. "This whole wedding thing, work, the cult thing, Alyssa and the baby..." I drew my hands to my mouth at my slip up. I'd agreed to keep Alyssa's secret, and in less than twenty-four hours, I'd already screwed up. "Don't tell Alyssa I told you. Gabe doesn't even know yet."

Mike's expression softened, and he moved to sit next to me on the rumpled comforter and put his arm around me. "I can't imagine there's much more to plan. I can deal with my groomsmen. You've already dealt with the dresses, the cake, the invitations, the flowers - what else could there possibly be?"

I held out my hand in front of me, realizing how badly I needed a manicure. I began counting them off on my fingers. "My dress, these nails, wedding favors, bridal shower, table decorations, ceremony technicalities, vows..."

He covered my hand with his. "Okay, point taken. Maybe you should take some time off in the afternoons. You have paid vacation accrued already. You can do a lot of work from home. With Alyssa, well, I don't know why you're worrying about that."

I interrupted. "I'm going to have to plan a baby shower!"

"That's months away judging by the looks of her, isn't it?"

With a nod, I relented. "Yeah, it is, but it's still something I need to deal with at some point. I really was hoping we could get this dress thing done and out of the way so we could start working on the cult case."

More than anything - I wanted to be done with that as soon as possible, but I knew infiltrating a cult was going to take longer than a couple of days. I knew Mike thought – or hoped - we were just going to give the FBI some information based on my knowledge of the occult, and that that would be that. Our luck just wasn't that good.

From downstairs, we heard the clatter of the racks as they were moved into the foyer and then Beverly's voice, a shrill cry above the calamity, echoed up the stairs. "Michael? Elizabeth?"

Mike groaned and got up. "Stay here. I'll see everyone out. I'll use the excuse of bad Chinese food."

He closed the door behind him as he left, leaving me in the cool silence of the bedroom. I fell back onto the bed. "Lucifuge? What's our first step?"

Aside from continued work on your astral magick skills, the main thing we need to do is bring you to the attention of one of the group's recruiters, and I know exactly the guy for that. Lucifuge sounded matter of fact, like he had it all planned out, for which I was grateful.

Am I going to have to kill anyone? I asked inwardly.

No, he said.

So, we're really just going in to gather evidence to take back to the FBI so they can take them down?

I felt Lucifuge hesitate. *Yes. You're more believable. An FBI infiltrator would be quickly discovered.*

Are you going to tell me the rest of it? My tone bordered on threatening.

More hesitation from the Daemon. *I can't explain it. You have to see it.*

That was an outright lie. I could feel it with every fiber of my being.

He sensed my flare of anger before I could even say anything. *I will tell you when the time is right.*

"I'm not a fan of going in blind," I whispered under my breath.

It's not the type of thing you can prepare for, he said.

Great, I thought. *If you were trying to curb my anxiety and make me more amiable, you're doing a crappy job.*

We start tomorrow afternoon. This guy doesn't even crawl out of bed until noon or later.

"Fabulous," I said aloud.

But the Daemon was gone and once again I was left alone with my thoughts. There was nothing left to do except retreat to my office to get some work done. Perhaps I could get enough done so that Kirk wouldn't mind me taking some time. In the meantime, I'd have to call Beverly and ask her if she could deal with some of the smaller decisions without me. I'd use a heavy work schedule as an excuse. Secure that I had a strategy, I got up and went downstairs to tell Mike my plan, relieved that Beverly, her entourage, and the racks of bridesmaids' dresses were gone. The strange thing was, compared to everything else on my plate - my wedding and my soon-to-be mother-in-law, my never-ending job, and the inevitable baby shower - Drakaris Deathspell seemed like child's play.

CHAPTER 7

L ucifuge left me alone during work the following day but showed up just as I pulled into the driveway at two in the afternoon. This time I didn't feel him ahead of time. *Let's get started,* he said out of the blue.

I jumped and paused for a moment to still my thumping heart. I was beginning to think I was going crazy, hearing a Daemon in my head. If it hadn't been for Mike, Alyssa, and Gabe all confirming the possession, I might have checked myself into the local hospital for a psych hold. "Don't jump into my mind like that," I scolded him as I unlocked the front door and stepped over the threshold. The house, smelling distinctly of cinnamon apple thanks to some air fresheners I kept just inside the door, had a definite calm about it, and I breathed in the solitude and comfort of home.

Sorry, the Daemon said, but he didn't feel sorry. Not to my psychic senses at least. Instead, his presence felt agitated and anxious, like a horse being held back when it wanted to bolt.

"I've been thinking," I said aloud. It was pointless to keep the conversation in my head when no one else was around - unless you counted Midnight, who was stretched out on the couch, napping. "I still don't understand why you chose me for this. I mean, I get I could fake the whole cult follower thing better than someone from the FBI, but why not some other practitioner? Maybe a magician better at astral magick?"

Admittedly, the astral magick sessions we'd been slipping in thirty minutes here and there weren't promising. I still wasn't *seeing* and *feeling* like he wanted me to, and I felt like I was letting Lucifuge down.

A lot of reasons, he said. *First, we have a rapport. Second, you're strong and you don't back down from a fight. Lastly, you're curious. You want to see what's going on and you are genuinely interested in helping me.*

My confidence sank to the pit of my stomach, and I suddenly felt vulnerable and emotional. "Great. Did you ever consider that I'm terrified of terrorists?"

Everyone's terrified of terrorists. Lucifuge tried to push into my body so he could make his way to the fridge.

"Hey. Knock it off, please. I'm not hungry." I stood fast and kept the Daemon out.

Lucifuge relented. *Fine. The first thing we need to do is some recon. So, call Mike and let him know we're going to do that. We just have to go down to that coffee shop off of 36th and Dayton.*

A knot started to twist in my throat. I could already hear Mike having a fit on the phone, insisting I wait until we met with Mike's friend, Stan, who was with the local FBI office. Mike had already invited Stan over to the house after he got off of work.

Call him, the Daemon persisted.

"Fine," I said. Begrudgingly, I picked up the phone and dialed Mike's number. It rang twice before he answered. "Hey babe," I started, hoping my lovable disposition would gain me some latitude.

"Is everything okay?" He sounded concerned.

I should have known better. It was rare for me to call him during the workday unless it was important. Usually, I just texted him so he could get back to me in his own time. My stomach knotted because I knew what was coming. There was no point in holding back because Mike wasn't going to like it no matter how hard I tried to soften the blow. "Yeah, everything's fine, but Lucifuge and I were thinking that we'd go out for coffee and maybe meet someone who knows someone on the inside of this group."

There was a long silence on the other end of the phone. I knew he was trying to think of the right words to avoid putting his foot in his mouth. I decided to take the opportunity to get myself out of the reprimand I knew was coming. "I know you would prefer that I didn't do this without some kind of backup, but Lucifuge assures me that this guy is perfectly safe and is in no way involved in the cult." My stomach rumbled with anxiety. I hated lying to him, but I saw no other way to keep the peace.

More silence.

"Mike?"

"I'm here. You're right, I don't like it. What if it's a trap? What if…"

"I trust Lucifuge." I hoped the finality in my voice would ease his mind and put a stop to this whole conversation.

Mike groaned. "Well, I guess I should just be thankful that you decided to call me and let me in on your plan this time around. Which coffee shop?"

I imagined him pulling out his notepad and the silver executive retractable alloy pen I'd gotten him for his birthday, ready to jot down the address.

This was the easy part because every witch, occultist, and ceremonial magician in the Denver Metro area knew where The Alchemist's Cupboard was. It was one of the hottest coffee shops in Northwest Denver. "Thirty-sixth and Dayton, The Alchemist's Cupboard. You may have heard of it?"

Mike snorted. "Got it, smart ass. Is your cell phone charged?"

"Yes." I pulled my cell phone out of my pocket and looked at the battery icon, relieved when I saw that it had a full charge. At least I wasn't lying to him about that.

"Make sure you have your tactical pen on you and the mace on your keychain. Don't go anywhere with anyone and stay away from the bathrooms. When you leave, make sure you're not being followed. I want a text when you get there, and I will call you fifteen minutes after I receive that text. You give me the code word if you need backup. You got that?" Mike's voice teetered on the edge of an argument.

"Got it," I said. I rummaged through my purse to make sure the mace and tactical pen were still there. They were. Ever since my last altercation, Mike had come up with a plan that I was supposed to follow if I ever found myself in danger. We'd agreed that I wouldn't go nosing around by myself, and if I found myself in a situation where I was alone, there was a system in place where he could get help to me if I needed it. He'd also insisted on being able to track me through my phone. A lot of couples might have fought over something like that, but I didn't put up a fight. If I owed Mike nothing else, I at least owed him that. I'd scared him enough times in the past year that he had a legitimate reason to be worried, and I knew it wasn't because he didn't trust me. It wasn't because he was controlling or obsessive. Mike genuinely worried because he knew I was too curious for my own damn good and that curiosity invariably threw me into some rough situations. So, I'd agreed without argument or complaint. Besides, it felt good knowing someone had my back. I knew he was probably already watching my phone and would continue to do so until I texted, just to make sure I made it safely. If it made him felt better - I didn't mind.

With a resigned sigh, he said, "Good. Be careful and tell that damn Daemon if he puts you in danger, I'm going to kick his ass."

I laughed. "He doesn't have an ass to kick unless he's in my body. Oh," I paused, trying to summon Lucifuge to me. "And the name of the guy we're meeting is…"

Gary, Lucifuge said. *Calls himself Maleficarus.*

Of course, he does, I thought, rolling my eyes. "The guy's name is Gary," I told Mike, leaving out the painfully trite poseur name Gary had given himself.

"Okay. And Liz," Mike said, his voice growing softer. "Watch your back and don't do anything stupid, okay? I also want you to text when you leave. I love you."

I'd never been one for sappiness, but I liked it when it came from Mike. "I love you too. And don't worry, I'll be really careful, I promise."

I hung up the phone and let out the deep breath I'd been subconsciously holding. "You better not get me into any trouble," I told Lucifuge.

Don't worry about it. I need you, right? Lucifuge's tone had that pragmatic, matter-of-fact feeling to it.

I nodded in agreement. It seemed reasonable the Daemon wouldn't want me to come into any harm, especially if he needed me.

There you have it then. I have no intention of allowing anything bad to happen to you. Trust me. The Daemon went silent then as I grabbed my jacket and bag, and the keys to my car. At this time of day, getting to The Alchemist's Cupboard would take about twenty minutes. I just wanted to get this done and over with as quickly and as painlessly as possible. A nagging doubt washed over me, and I took a deep breath before leaving the house. *Trust me* was a phrase used all too often by con men, hucksters, and used car salesman when they were about to screw you over.

The Alchemist's Cupboard sat on the corner of a rundown strip mall. The parking lot had seen better days and was full of potholes and dead weeds. I parked in what I assumed was a parking space, denoted by a crumbling parking block. The only thing separating the parking lot from the houses behind it was an expanse of dead greenbelt area.

There were five other cars there, but Lucifuge seemed certain that Gary would be among those lounging at one of the tables on a weekday afternoon when most people were at work. Secure in the knowledge that the Daemon was within me, I got out of the car and hurried through the brisk afternoon air into the coffee shop, sliding up to the empty counter to get café mocha at Lucifuge's request. The kid behind the counter barely acknowledged me, but quickly rang up my order and told me to have a seat. He'd bring it out to me shortly. Not once did he look me in the eye.

I turned and surveyed the small shop, immediately drawn to a balding, portly man with a full beard sitting at a corner table, looking at his phone.

That's the guy, Lucifuge said.

Well, I can't just walk up to him and say, hey, you're Gary, right? That wouldn't be too suspicious, I thought.

Sit at the table next to him. I'll take care of the rest, Lucifuge assured me.

I did as Lucifuge suggested, then pulled out my phone to quickly text Mike, so he knew I was there. I checked to make sure the ringer was on so I could answer his safety phone call, and then continued the ruse of pretending to be engrossed in my phone. From the corner of my eye, I noticed Gary looking at me. He cocked his head to one side, looking at… my chest? I looked down to find a large silver inverse pentagram around my neck, and my previously blue blouse was now black.

I had to make some modifications, Lucifuge said wryly. *You're not really Christian Satanist bait without the glam.*

"Great," I murmured under my breath. I lifted my eyes and found them locked in Gary's gaze. He smiled. I smiled and looked back down at my phone. *Gods, what did you do to me?*

Good, you've piqued his interest. I could almost feel the Daemon luring the man. *He's coming over.*

Lucifuge was right. Gary was, indeed, heading over to the table with his coffee and a ratty messenger bag in tow.

"Do you mind if I sit with you?" he asked, his voice a lot less menacing than his biker look.

"Umm…" I shrugged. Just as I motioned to Gary to take a seat, the barista brought my coffee and set it in front of me without so much as a word. But I was thankful for the distraction because it gave me a moment to recover.

"I'm Gary, but my friends call me Maleficarus." He reached a stubby hand across the table.

I took it into my own and shook. "I'm Sharon."

"It's nice to meet you, Sharon. I noticed the star of Satan," Gary said, nodding to my new glam jewelry, courtesy Lucifuge.

I brought my hand up to pentacle protectively and said, "It was blessed by the Daemon Lucifuge."

Gary's eyebrow went up in surprise and his smile widened. "So, you are aligned with the Master's work."

"I would certainly hope so," I said, feigning mild offense.

"It's so nice to run into brothers and sisters in service to His Majesty's infernal glory," Gary said before taking a sip of his coffee.

Real people don't talk like this, I screamed in my mind. I could feel Lucifuge's amusement. Outwardly, I smiled. "Well, I am a vessel of Lucifuge."

Good, Lucifuge said. *You've got him.*

"I take it Lucifuge is your Guardian Daemon?" Gary gave me an expectant look, then peered into his near empty coffee cup. "Hold that thought while I get another cup."

He got up and in three strides, was at the counter ordering another coffee.

What now? I asked inwardly.

Just go with your intuition. You're doing great, Lucifuge said, his voice filled with encouragement.

When Gary returned, I stalled by sipping on the Latte. With each steaming sip, I could feel the Daemon enjoying what he considered an earthly delight. Perhaps coffee in itself was a deadly sin. *No,* I thought, *it probably falls under gluttony.*

"You looked perplexed," Gary said, folding his hands on the table in front of him.

"I was just debating if coffee fell under one of the deadly sins. Lucifuge loves Mocha Latte." I knew how crazy it sounded when it fell from my lips, but I said it with conviction because I could be completely honest with this guy, and he was devout enough to not think I was crazy. Or he was crazy enough to play along.

Or fooled into believing you're crazy enough to join a cult, Lucifuge chimed in.

Gary's smile had grown to Cheshire cat proportions, and it dawned on me that Lucifuge was probably right. It made sense that someone recruiting for a cult would look for the most vulnerable - the emotionally compromised, the mentally unstable. Those would be the people who found acceptance in a cult and were more likely to allow someone else to control and manipulate them with promises of power, or love, or whatever that person desired.

Gary's silence and lack of information divulging were starting to annoy me, though. I didn't want to play games. "And who is your Guardian Daemon?"

"I answer only to Satan himself. Praise His name," Gary said, bowing his head in manufactured humility.

"It's unfortunate there are no proper temples for those of us in service to Him," I said wistfully, throwing in a dreamy gaze out the window before taking another sip of coffee. That's when I noticed my nails were longer than usual and painted black. Before I could spend too much time contemplating how Lucifuge had managed to change my appearance without me, or anyone else for that matter, noticing, Gary lifted his hands and clapped them together.

"That's where you're wrong, sister. There is a group, but they are very selective in who they allow in. I'm afraid only the chosen are given entrance. They have to be approved by the Master Himself." He immediately shut up when he noticed the barista bringing him his coffee. Once the young man had left, Gary leaned across the table toward me and lowered his voice. "But the great Dark Warlock Sethial and the High Priest may grant you audience if I put in a good word for you."

"And what would that cost me?" I narrowed my eyes and shot him a wicked smile.

"You know the price," he said, waggling an eyebrow.

My phone rang. I'd never felt such relief in my life. "Excuse me, I have to take this. It's my asshole boss."

"You good?" Mike's voice sounded in my ear, and I turned down the volume a few notches just to make sure Gary couldn't eavesdrop.

"Yeah, I got it. I'll bring it in with me tomorrow." I looked at Gary and shook my head, rolling my eyes.

He snickered.

"Text me before you leave or nine-one-one if anything happens. You want another call?" Mike asked.

You won't need one. We'll be leaving in fifteen minutes, Lucifuge said. The Daemon's voice sent a feeling of dead calm through me.

"I'll be in fifteen minutes early, no need to give me a wakeup call. But if you want, I'll call you before I leave," I said, trying to make my voice sound detached and impersonal.

"You're leaving in fifteen minutes?" Mike asked. Thank gods he wasn't thick.

"Yes. I already have what you wanted me to pick up. Okay, Mr. Carson?" I shot an apologetic smile to Gary, who patiently sipped his coffee and listened to my one-sided conversation.

"Okay, bye," Mike said.

"Goodbye, Mr. Carson." I tapped the call off and shook my head, then looked at Gary. "My mortal boss, Mr. Carson, who's all of eighty-five and helpless sometimes."

"It's unfortunate we have to continue to exist in this mortal coil and serve human masters. And for what?" Gary's eyes pierced me, dark gray and scanning.

"Well, I suppose until Master Satan can afford to care for me on this earthly plane, I'm stuck working for a human master," I whispered with a sigh.

"Now back to our conversation," Gary said.

I forced a smile. I suddenly had an idea how to handle Gary. I lowered my voice. "Ah yes, I take it you're looking for sex in exchange for a group invite," I said with a coy smile. "While it sounds tempting as you're quite attractive, I'm afraid I'll have to decline. I am a servant betrothed to the horned god Himself. Only our Master Satan or any Daemon he decrees may penetrate my flesh, and only during ritual. So says the blood pact that I made with Our Dark Lord."

"That's some dedication. A physical specimen of beauty like you, it makes sense The Dark Lord would keep you for his own delight. Perhaps I'll talk to the leaders of the group anyway. I can't guarantee anything, but I imagine once they see you and feel the presence of Satan that permeates you, they might agree to speak to Satan on your behalf and bring you into the group. It will be up to Drakaris Deathspell." He said that name as if it should have carried all the weight in the world.

I acted dumb. "Who?"

"The One. The High Priest of Satan who will usher in the coming of the Anti-Christ and the prophecies foretold in Revelations." Gary must have believed what he was saying because he said it with a great deal of conviction. Or maybe he was just a good actor. I was beginning to think I wasn't so bad at acting myself.

I sat for a moment and finished the coffee in my cup. "I don't know. Sounds too good to be true, if you know what I mean."

"Could we have dinner sometime later this week?" Gary cocked his head to one side again, like a curious puppy. "I mean, I'd have to get to know you a bit better before approaching the heads of The Antichrist's Temple. Believe me – you want in on this."

I shrugged. "I don't know, maybe. We could have dinner to talk about it some more. But I'd want to know more before I committed. There are so many groups out there that just want to do sex magick, and I don't want to break my blood oath for that."

"I assure you we're the real deal. Not like those poseur groups out there," Gary said. In his voice, I heard a slight tinge of worry. Worry that he'd lost my interest for good.

"Well, checking them out goes both ways, so..." I persisted.

Good, play hard to get. He likes a challenge, Lucifuge said.

Gary's hand shot out and covered mine. "Give me your number. We'll have dinner. You won't regret it."

"Oh, um, sure. I don't have a card or anything..."

Gary pulled his hands away from me and reached into his bag, pulling out a pen and notepad.

I gave him my number, then looked at my phone. "Oh, I suppose I should get going. I have to meet my landlady for an inspection."

I got up to go. "It was good to meet you, Gary. I'm looking forward to hearing from you."

He stood and took my left hand into his, gently lifting it and kissing the back of it. "It was a pleasure. You'll hear from me soon."

I groaned inwardly. Outwardly, I managed a nod and a little wave, and then I high tailed it out of there, got in the car, and drove away as quickly as possible.

"Gods, that was a nightmare," I told Lucifuge. "How long do I have to spend with this guy, and will he always talk like that?"

Calm yourself, Elizabeth. Lucifuge sent a sense of calm through me.

"I shouldn't have had the coffee," I whispered. Halfway home I pulled over to text Mike since I'd forgotten to text him in the parking lot. No doubt, he'd been watching my phone's progress toward home. In my mind, I went over the conversation with Gary, and before I realized it, I was pulling into the driveway. Mike, along with a man I could only assume was FBI Stan, stood on the front porch waiting for me.

It was hard to believe, just by looking at him, that FBI Stan was one of the many men and women tasked to keep people safe from terrorist threats. Tall, slender, and not a day over thirty, he looked harmless, with short cropped brown hair.

Actually, he reminded me of a Mormon missionary with the black pants and dress shoes, and the crisp white shirt. The only thing missing was the tie and backpack. It wasn't until Stan opened his mouth that one could tell he was in law enforcement. That was always a dead giveaway. There were certain words and phrases cops used more frequently in usual conversation that normal people didn't. Like referring to people as an *accessory* or *suspect* or saying someone had a *fair knowledge of* an incident, and everything was *alleged.* Since Mike and I had begun our relationship, I'd been around more policemen, detectives, and FBI agents than most people, and the dead giveaway was always in how they spoke and carried themselves.

We made our way into the house and straight to the dining room. Everyone sat. FBI Stan leaned across the table toward me as I told him and Mike about my meeting with Gary, carefully leaving out Lucifuge's commentary and involvement. When I was done, Stan turned to Mike and a slow smile spread across his thin lips. "I have to agree. We have to let her go in."

Mike bit his lower lip. "Yeah. Well, she knows the community and the type of people we're dealing with, that's for sure. But I can't say yes to that unless you can assure me that she'll be safe." He turned to Stan with a questioning look, setting his jaw.

"We have new tech where we can add wires to everything from shampoo bottles to shoes, and even hair barrettes with no one being any the wiser." Then Stan turned to me. "How smart do you think these guys are?"

I traced my finger over the handle of my teacup and chuckled. "Well, considering their unimaginative temple name and their stereotypical monikers, I seriously doubt they're the type who will be checking me out for wires. Especially in my shampoo or shoes, or even clothes, unless they're trying to get me out of them for a Satanic orgy. Besides – I'm pretty sure I've convinced Gary I'm crazy enough to follow their little temple."

Stan's eyes popped open and his jaw dropped slightly at my utterance of the word orgy. It was likely his equivalent to pearl clutching.

"These guys, or at least this Gary, is a Christian Satanist. That means they do everything Christians think Satanists do, often because they're rebelling against the religion they were raised in. They like the dark, scary image. They like scaring Christians by being what Christians fear most. They're not like normal Satanists," I explained with a shrug.

"Normal Satanists?" Stan leaned in toward me again, his raised eyebrows and wide eyes begging to know more.

"Normal Satanists view Satan as an archetype for knowledge and free-will. Some may believe in spirits, others are atheists, but they don't go out of their way to fulfill a stereotype. They don't go by ridiculous names, or dress all in black, or try to bring about Armageddon or the Anti-Christ ala *The Omen*. Most of them are just normal people who believe in themselves and their own power over that of any alleged god," I said, standing. I needed more tea. "Of course, I think I should talk to Gary more and get him to introduce me to Stone and the other guy before we start making big plans. We have to consider that."

"Who did you say Benjamin Stone's accessory was again?" Stan flipped through his notes.

"He goes by the name Dark Warlord Sethial. The *i-a-l* at the end suggests, to me anyway, that he likely considers himself some sort of dark justice angel." I didn't even bother trying to hide my disdain. After plopping a new tea bag into my highly inappropriate *Eat a Bag of Dicks* cup, I poured hot water from the dark blue ceramic kettle over it, inhaling the fragrance of my favorite orange pekoe and black Assam blend.

"So," Mike said, leaning back. "We start wiring her starting the next meeting."

Stan nodded.

Right on cue, my phone rang, vibrating angrily against the dining table. Mike picked it up. "Unknown number. Local."

My stomach twisted with knowing. In two exaggerated strides, I made it across the kitchen to the table and grabbed it from Mike's hand. I answered, putting a finger to my lips as if they needed any prompting to shut up. "Hello?"

"Sharon?"

"Yes."

"It's Maleficarus. We met at the Alchemist's Cupboard earlier?" He paused with uncertainty. "I know it probably seems a bit bold, me calling only a few hours after the fact, but I'd really like to schedule dinner."

"Oh, um, let me look at my calendar." I pursed my lips together, waiting until a suitable time had passed. "I have a few hours tomorrow night and…"

Before I could get the rest of the sentence out of my mouth, Gary jumped in. "Tomorrow night would be fantastic. Can I pick you up?"

"It would be easier if we just met somewhere. Did you have a place in mind?" I cringed a little, hoping I didn't sound too suspicious. Mike and Stan sat, with bated breath, waiting.

Gary gave me the address, a small brew pub only a few blocks away from The Alchemist's Cupboard, seven o'clock tomorrow night. I hung up with the sweetest goodbye I could muster and took a deep breath. "Tomorrow night. Pub Five."

"I know the place," Mike said, narrowing his eyes. "Yuppie joint. It doesn't seem like his crowd if he's some dark and scary Christian Satanist."

Mike had a point. That was an odd choice. The heavy Daemonic presence of Lucifuge filled the room.

It was a test, Lucifuge said.

"A test?" I said aloud, my hand immediately moving to my mouth when I realized the error.

"What do you mean a test?" Stan asked, exchanging a glance with Mike.

"Damn it. I think it was a test. To see if I'd protest the yuppie brew pub." I groaned inwardly.

Don't worry, Lucifuge assured me. *When you meet him there tomorrow, before going in, request something less trendy. Or text him beforehand. I'm sure there's some alternative hole in the wall you could direct him to.*

With a brisk nod, I said, "I need to find something more alternative, goth-like. Unique. Same neighborhood. I'll just text him beforehand and change the location. Suggestions?"

Stan and Mike exchanged glances again.

I put my hands on my hips and gave them a wide smile. "Well, guys, you better get to work. We need a new location, a plan, and all the equipment to wire me in place before seven tomorrow night. Now, who wants pizza?"

A rush of excitement and adrenaline ran through me. *I would like some pizza,* Lucifuge said.

CHAPTER 8

I chose a small Pho restaurant in yet another strip mall about a mile from the original brew pub. Not surprisingly, Gary seemed pleased I'd chosen something different, making me certain it was another test. He wore a long black trench coat, black jeans, and a black shirt, and tonight - he also wore black eyeliner. Around his neck, he sported three amulets. One, the typical inverted pentagram, layered atop an inverted cross, and after that - a seal of Lucifer. A sure sign someone was trying too hard, or at least that was always my first impression. I'd learned over the years some of the most hardcore magicians and dedicants didn't wear much in the way of amulets at all, unless they were doing a ritual. I fought the urge to roll my eyes.

We ordered our drinks and noodle bowls and then found ourselves in a moment of uncomfortable silence.

"I'm glad you chose this. I wasn't sure what your scene was." When he said that, he motioned to my outfit.

I had worn a simple black shirt, a pair of jeans, and my favorite black canvas slip-on shoes, along with Mike and Stan's carefully hidden microphones. But again, Lucifuge had changed my appearance, and now I had on a tight bodice shirt that pushed my cleavage to heaving, and tight black pants complimented by heeled suede booties. I also wore a single amulet, a silver sigil of Lucifuge which I rather liked.

You can keep it, Lucifuge had told me after I'd first seen it and thought about how neat it was. *Perhaps Daemons weren't half bad as fashion stylists, after all,* I thought. He certainly had a better aesthetic eye for clothing than I did.

I looked at Gary and shrugged. "I don't really have a scene. I just do what I like to do and go where I feel like going." It sounded far more apathetic than I meant it to.

Gary leaned forward across the table, his hands folded in front of him. "So, what do you like to do in your free time?"

Ah, this was part of the interview, I thought.

Of course, it is, Lucifuge quipped.

"I am not overly social, so mostly I spend time in my temple or reading," I said. It wasn't a complete lie. I was an introvert by my very nature, and never understood why society tried to push all introverts toward extroversion at every turn.

"You just haven't met the right people. People who are as dedicated as you to our Dark Lord and His Daemons." He immediately stopped talking when a young Asian man paused at our table and set down a bottle of Sriracha, then checked our drinks to make sure we didn't need refills.

"So, what about you?" I wanted to get more information out of him, otherwise being wired was pointless. One thing about wires is they're nothing like in the movies. I was wired to broadcast everything said back to Mike and Stan, who along with a handful of FBI agents, two who were sitting three booths away, could hear everything I said. But I couldn't hear them or receive direction.

You have me for that, Lucifuge said.

"I frequent a few clubs, but I mostly keep to our own kind." Gary forced a smile, and in that moment, I could tell he was sizing me up. I felt like a gazelle in a lion's gaze.

I wasn't too keen about phrases like *our own kind*, but I went with it. I leaned forward and lowered my voice, hoping Mike and Stan could still hear me. "Most of the people I meet are poseurs. They don't know the true power of Satan. So how is it you found the only group of non-poseurs?"

"Well, I'm not an introvert. On the contrary, I am very active in the local community, and I agree with you. The majority of them are atheists with a bone to pick. Not actual followers of the Dark Lord. But our King uses them all the same, so we tolerate them." Gary gave me a knowing smile.

"To what end? As a distraction?" Just then, our waiter brought out the platter with two heaping bowls of Pho.

Once the waiter had gone, Gary began poking at his Pho. "They serve His purpose in their own way. It's not for us to judge The Dark Lord's wisdom."

I almost snorted. Then I felt it, that familiar sensation of Lucifuge climbing into my body. *This smells really good,* the Daemon said. He pushed my consciousness partially to the back of my mind so I could still see and hear, but it was Lucifuge controlling the conversation now, and it was more than him just wanting a bite of my Pho.

"We need to just cut the shit and get to the point, Gary," my voice, but deeper and grating, said.

Gary flew backward against the bench of the booth and stared at me in horror, his jaw slack. The agents a few booths away glanced over, one of them moved to get out of the booth, but sat back down, probably by order. Gary swallowed, hard.

"Relax, Gary," Lucifuge said, picking up the chopsticks and expertly maneuvering them in the bowl of Pho to capture the rice noodles. He took a bite. "This is good. One of the things so many humans don't savor as much as they should. The flavor is amazing."

Gary looked around, then back at me. "She really is possessed..."

"Of course, she is. She's one of Satan's chosen, and I'm her patron. I have full use of her body as I see fit. Now, let's cut the crap. I need to talk with Drakaris and Sethial. Satan wants Sharon to be a part of the plan. She's one of our favorites." Lucifuge took another mouthful of noodles, this time with a slice of beef.

I could only imagine that Lucifuge was doing the red eye thing, because why else would a guy like Gary, allegedly a dedicant of Satan, freak out over a possession?

Oh, give me a break. The first real glimpse at the Daemonic and most of these people would shit their pants and go sprinting back to Jesus, Lucifuge said inwardly.

Gary took a long time to respond. Finally, in a small voice, he said, "Yes, Master. I will contact both Drakaris and Sethial and arrange for them to grant you an audience."

"As I see it," Lucifuge paused long enough to pick up a glass of iced tea. He took a sip, wrinkling his nose with a frown and set it back down. "I'm the one granting them the audience."

Sitting back, watching it all as an observer, I couldn't help but feel like I was watching a B horror flick. The sudden lack of confidence in Gary's face was smacking of a man who'd just been put in his place.

Lucifuge didn't stop there. He seemed to enjoy tormenting the ridiculous man before him. "Perhaps you should be a good little minion and call them now. I don't have the patience to play games. I have plenty of other things, more interesting things, to do."

"Of course," Gary fumbled in his trench coat pocket and pulled out his phone. "I'll just step outside..." He started to get up, but stopped, fear entering his eyes as an unseen force prevented him from moving.

"You'll do it right here."

"Someone could overhear..." Gary started in protest.

Lucifuge held up my carefully manicured hand, manicured by Daemonic magick, not me, and pointed a long black nail at him. "I insist."

With another gulp, Gary found the number on his phone and made the call. "Sethial, it's Maleficarus. I need you to meet with someone. He… she insists."

A long pause, with Gary glancing at Lucifuge, obviously nervous.

After an uncomfortable ten minutes, Gary finally hung up, having secured the meeting for the following week.

"Now," Lucifuge said with sharp precision, "I think we have nothing further to discuss. You've served my purpose. We'll reconvene in a week." Then Lucifuge and I stood, and with a sly smile, turned from the table and strode out the door. By the time I'd reached the walkway outside, I was once again in full faculty of my body.

You do realize the FBI heard that whole thing, I scolded him inwardly.

They'll just think you're a great actress, Lucifuge said. I could almost feel him giving me a smug shrug.

I rolled my eyes and made my way to the car, purposefully ignoring the white van two spots over. When I finally pulled out of the parking lot, I saw Gary still inside the restaurant in my rearview, just getting up to leave.

Mike and Stan, along with their throng of four additional agents whose names I didn't know, arrived at our house fifteen minutes after me. It was enough time for me to change into a comfortable sweatshirt and jeans. How was I going to explain the change of clothing? The goth make-up? I'd have to make it up on the fly.

"Here she is," Mike said when he led the five agents into the living room. "Great acting, babe."

I nodded.

Stan shook his head in mock disbelief. "How did you know he would fall for the possessed act?"

I shrugged, somehow managing to remain nonchalant even though my insides were quivering with anxiety. "I know the type. Proselytizing, evangelical Satanists are all alike. The males of the species have some unrealistic sex magick fap fantasy that resembles a cheesy ass Gor novel."

The agents all furrowed their brows.

"Some writer from the late sixties wrote this series of novels where women were just men's playthings. Add Daemons, some sadism and bondage, along with a lot of gullibility and sexual desperation, and that's these guys pegged in a nutshell." I exchanged a knowing smile with Mike and I could swear I saw him breathe a sigh of relief.

"I wonder if that would have worked if you were a man?" one of the agents, the tall, blond forty-something, who stood six inches over the rest of them, asked.

I shook my head. "Probably not. I think Gary is easily manipulated by women, even though he dominates them in his fantasies."

This comment was met with chuckles and the tall blond blushed.

"You guys want some coffee? Tea?" I asked, moving to get up from the couch.

They all agreed on coffee, and I retreated to the kitchen to make a pot. The anxiety in the pit of my stomach subsided. I could hear the guys talking but didn't bother to eavesdrop. I was too tired. Hosting a Daemon took a toll on a person, and I felt like I'd just ran a marathon. As I filled the coffee cups, I snickered at the thought of all the people online who claimed to be possessed all the time. *If they only knew*, I thought.

When the coffee was ready, I carefully set them on the tray we often used to serve coffee or tea when Beverly came to visit, and carried it to the living room, finding the guys leaning inward toward the small tape recorder on the coffee table.

"Did you hear that?" tall guy asked.

"Yeah, what is that?" Stan asked, stopping the recording, cranking the volume, and hitting play again.

This time, I heard it, too. I could hear Gary talking, recalling it was the conversation he had with Drakaris on the phone.

"The bridge must be closed, soon," snarled the low, grating voice in the recorder.

Then there was another voice, and this one I recognized. "It will be done," said Lucifuge, this time in his own voice and not mine.

I felt the blood rush from my face. "Ugh, Pho," I said, setting the tray on the table, which garnered attention from the entire room. "I apologize if this is rude, but I think I need to go lay down until my stomach settles."

Mike stood as if he wanted to help.

"No, I'll be okay," I assured him before slipping out of the room and making my way upstairs to the bedroom. Once inside, I closed the door and pressed my back against it, squeezing my eyes shut. "Well, that wasn't so subtle," I whispered harshly, hoping Lucifuge heard me.

He didn't respond.

With an exaggerated groan, I flopped myself on to the bed, face first into my pillow, only to surface to find two green cat eyes watching me from Mike's side of the bed. "Don't judge me," I said to Midnight. Then I rolled over and closed my eyes.

I woke to the horrifying realization that I'd missed a wedding meeting-thingy with Beverly and Kenny DeBeers. I was upright in a flash, and the moment my socked feet hit the floor, it took only two strides to the bedroom door. I flung open it open and started over the threshold, smacking right into Mike's chest. I would have fallen on my ass if he hadn't reached out to steady me.

"Where's the fire?" He looked around as if he expected to see a grotesque monster chasing me.

"I think I forgot some wedding thing with your mom and Kenny, gods damn it!" My eyes frantically flew past him. I had to get to my appointment book downstairs.

"Calm down. You didn't miss anything. That's tomorrow morning. Besides, Stan's still here."

"It's still night?"

Mike laughed, then lowered his voice. "You've only been asleep for about an hour and a half. The other guys just left.

"Oh gods." I hand flew to my forehead and I shoved my auburn locks away from my face. "The voices…"

With a quick shake of his dark head of hair, Mike leaned into me and whispered, "They think they had some static or interference over the line. We all agreed it was creepy, but you shouldn't read into that. Stan says these devices do that sometimes. The wireless picks up another conversation, distorts voices. That probably explains some EVP phenomenon, too," he said.

I narrowed my eyes and frowned at him. Always the skeptic looking for a scientific explanation, but then maybe he was right. Perhaps I was the one being superstitious. After all, Lucifuge didn't seem concerned about it. I was probably just overtired. "What time is it?"

"Nine, you want to go back to bed?"

I shook my head. "Not yet. I need some water and some ibuprofen or something." I squeezed my way past him and started down the stairs, hanging onto the railing because I was still pretty tired, and my heart still thumped in my chest from the panic that came from thinking I missed an important meeting with my mother-in-law to be. I could hear her now.

Elizabeth. How careless of you to forget such an important meeting for your own wedding. If I didn't know any better, I'd think you didn't want to marry my son at all.

By the time I'd reached the bottom step, I had scrunched my nose and was mouthing the words.

I turned toward the kitchen and came face to face with Stan, who was munching on an oatmeal cookie from the batch I'd made over the weekend.

He paused to swallow the food in his mouth before asking, "Feeling better?"

I forced my most pleasant smile and nodded. "Yeah, I don't think my stomach appreciated the Pho on top of all that anxiety of possibly being made by our friend Gary."

"You did a really good job. You're as good as in, with the Daemon on board, of course. How is that going to work exactly?" He didn't really seem to be asking me, because his eyes went up and left when he said it, as if it was one of the great questions of the universe.

I started toward the kitchen, motioning him to follow, "I'll just tell him that me and the Daemon are a package deal, but the Daemon comes out when necessary to give instruction."

It sounded like a lame plan to me, but Stan seemed to give me the benefit of the doubt. "Well, you know these people."

"So, what have you guys been doing down here for almost two hours?" I asked him over my shoulder as I filled my water glass from the tap.

"Just trying to convince your significant-other that we're not going to let anything happen to you, and that you're going into this with full backup and a connection."

I drank my water. That sounded about right.

"He feels like you'd be going in with no significant backup. But we do this kind of thing for a living, so he should know better." He glanced toward the staircase. "If it were anyone else, he'd probably trust me on this."

I nodded. "It doesn't help that I have a habit of getting into trouble. He's right to worry," I said. The last thing I wanted was Mike's friends razzing him about being worried about me.

Stan chuckled with a wide grin. "I've heard all about it. You're kind of a legend with this occult stuff. Hanson, the tall blond man who was here earlier, thinks you'd be a good profiler for suspects who practice the occults."

The way he said it was the same way someone's grandma might say *the internets*. I bit my inner lip to keep from laughing. "Maybe I should write a book."

"Not a bad idea," he shot back at me.

Just then, Mike strode back into the kitchen, and I was thankful I didn't have to explain that I'd only been joking about the writing a book thing.

I had just grabbed myself an oatmeal cookie when Stan said, "Liz, Mike, I should get going, but we're good and we'll meet next week to get you ready for this meeting. We'll lay out the game plan. We're going to catch these guys, and safely, too."

We said goodbye, and Mike walked him to the door, returning with his hands on his hips. "I don't like this. You have to promise me the second you feel like you're in over your head, Daemon or not, that you will get the hell out of Dodge."

"Like the wind," I said through a mouthful of cookie. I swallowed and washed it down with another mouthful of tap water. "You think I want to be in a dangerous situation? I'm only doing this because it can save innocent lives. I would feel horrible if people died because I was too chicken-shit to stand up to a few delusional assholes who think the Antichrist is coming."

"You see delusional Satanists; I see crazy bastards who would kill you." Mike moved over to me and put his hands on my shoulders. "I just have a bad feeling."

"Lucifuge promised he wouldn't let anything bad happen," I said, as if that was supposed to ease his mind. "Then why do I feel like the shit is going to hit the fan and that something is going to go horribly wrong?"

He pulled me into his arms and hugged me, tighter than he usually did.

CHAPTER 9

I stayed home the next two days to both deal with wedding plans and clean the house, because most of what I had to do at work didn't need to be done at the office. With video chat, I could connect with Kirk and my other co-workers at any time. I wish I could say my heart was in the planning of me and Mike's wedding, but it wasn't, and I could see that my feelings on the matter were reflected in my body language - by the way I crossed my arms over my chest or looked at the clock, or sighed when I was tired of waiting. I could also see it reflected in the terse looks from Beverly, often accompanied by the occasional head shake, but she said nothing. Thankfully.

I'd even started planning Alyssa's baby shower, seeking advice from websites run by women who made baby showers their life's calling. Aside from our thirty-minute astral sessions here and there, Lucifuge remained thankfully absent from my daily life. I needed the break, and for the first time in weeks, my skin didn't feel electrified and my stomach wasn't in knots. I'd stopped at a local party supply to look at party favors and ideas for Alyssa's shower even though I knew it was too soon. She still had over seven months to go, but I knew it would take me that long to plan and think things over. I wanted it to be perfect. I wanted to call her to ask how Gabe was taking the news but decided against it. It was only two in the afternoon and she was at work. It would have to wait, so in the meantime, I wandered to the wedding aisle and looked at the cheap balloons, plasticware, crepe paper, and other sundries that people who didn't have mothers-in-law like Beverly were more apt to buy for less formal affairs.

While I dreamed of an informal picnic wedding, perhaps something with costumes, or just jeans and t-shirts, I was completely oblivious to the man following me through the aisle. It didn't even occur to me that his trench coat, backward ball cap, and boots seemed a bit out of place for a guy meandering through the wedding aisle at Parties Plus. When I noticed him, I moved a few feet to the left in front of the ten-dollar cake toppers. An uneasy feeling gripped my gut when he took up space between us. I couldn't tell if he was watching me thanks to his dark sunglasses, but his facial expression was hard, his jaw set. Scraggly and greasy hair fell to his shoulder, likely unwashed for days.

I took another few steps away from him. He followed. My every instinct told me to run, but my rational mind told me I needed to find a store employee and make up a ton of questions just so I wasn't alone. I moved out of the aisle, my eyes searching for another live person. I spotted my intended target, a lone teenager wearing a blue smock, stocking bags of balloons on a shelf. I hurried toward him, though my legs felt like rubber.

"Excuse me," I called out, forcing a smile. "Do you have any wedding cake toppers with maybe just a heart?"

From the corner of my eye, I saw the man glance at me and start toward the front door. The kid in front of me said something about if it wasn't on the shelf then they didn't have it, but I wasn't listening. I turned and watched the man leave with one purposeful glance back at me. Once he'd passed through the automatic door, I breathed an audible sigh of relief.

"I think that guy was following me," I told the kid.

The young man's eyes went wide, and he followed my gaze to the door. I'd always heard of women being stalked in stores, but never thought I'd actually have it happen.

"Do you want me to call the police?" the kid asked, unsure. "I can get my manager."

"No, I just want to stay here for a few minutes and call my fiancé." I pulled my phone from my pocket, found Mike, and tapped his number. It took a few seconds, but the phone started ringing. "Let me just stand next to you for a few minutes until I collect myself," I told the kid.

The young man shrugged and cautiously began stocking the racks again, every so often looking back at me and then back at the store's entrance.

It went to voice mail - damn it. "Mike, it's Liz," as if I needed to say. "I'm at Parties Plus and some weird guy was following me through the store. I'm going to stay here for about fifteen minutes and then head home," I said into the phone. "Love you and see you later."

I hung up and gave the kid, who had stopped what he was doing to look at me again, a grateful smile. "Thanks."

"No problem."

I pointed back down the wedding aisle. "I'm going to just hang out and look at wedding stuff for a few." Then I smiled a genuine smile as I considered buying some cheap crepe paper and a plastic cake topper, just so I could hand them the Beverly and watch the look of sheer horror wash over her face. Not to mention it seemed only fair I should buy something if I was going to linger in the store until my nerves were calm. I finally settled on the tacky crucifix cake topper and a wedding guest book with llamas on it - one dressed as a bride, and the other as a groom. On the outside, in a sweeping cursive font, it said *Our Wedding Guest Book*. That would be sure to send Beverly to boil, especially since she had mentioned the leather-covered Guest Book she had in mind. I took my time and checked out about fifteen minutes later. Armed with my purse over my shoulder, my keys in one hand and the plastic Parties Plus bag in the other, I strode confidently to the parking lot toward my car.

The van pulled up quickly, and I was yanked into it so fast, that I dropped my shopping bag. It barely had time to register that I'd be snatched. When it finally did, the only words I could manage were, "What the fuck?"

"Drakaris Deathspell wants to see you. Now," biker guy said. Looking at him head-on, I recognized the bedraggled, aging metalhead from the store. His skin was weathered from too much time outside without sunscreen.

"You could have fucking asked instead of dragging me into your shitty van. Who are you?" I got into character, taking on the persona of Sharon. I wasn't dressed anything like the Sharon Maleficarus had encountered, and I began to worry that maybe that was a bad thing. *Lucifuge*, my mind called to him. Nothing. Damnit.

"I'm an acolyte. My name isn't important," he said. I peered around to the driver. It wasn't Maleficarus. Just some guy with a scruffy beard, bald head, and a dragon tattoo on the back of his neck. Acolyte nodded toward the driver. "He's an acolyte, too."

"How convenient." I folded my arms over my chest and tried to straighten myself on the floor of the now moving van. At least I still had my car keys and my purse, but the joke wedding guest book and the ridiculous cake topper were gone. I looked into the mirrored sunglasses of Acolyte One, the guy who'd stalked me in the store. "How long is this shit going to take? I was picking up a few things for a co-worker and I'm expected back at work in the next twenty minutes."

"It takes as long as it does," Acolyte One said.

The driver groaned. "Man, weren't you supposed to blindfold her or some shit?"

"I don't have a blindfold. Besides, she'll just take it off. She's the one who went out of her way into scaring Maleficarus into getting a meeting with Drakaris anyway." He took off his sunglasses and looked at me when he said that last bit. He should have left them on, flashing his green eyes at me wasn't the least bit intimidating. "You're not really possessed by a Daemon."

I laughed. "No, I'm not. It's not my fault Drakaris has wanna-be goths and metalheads as minions," I said, figuring that if Lucifuge wasn't going to show up, I had to have a backup plan. They already thought Maleficarus was a dumb ass, so I saw no harm in going with that.

"You should have brought a gag," the driver said over his shoulder.

"You should have asked," I repeated. "You can't even get into a Satanic group without all this bullshit? Whatever happened to just meeting at a diner like everyone else does it?"

Acolyte One snorted and shook his head but didn't say anything.

The drive wasn't long. About fifteen minutes along one of the main thoroughfares through town, heading south, to Lakewood, not five blocks from my old house which I was now renting to an older couple. They pulled up to a small corner house with a chain link fence around it. The yard was surprisingly well kept, as was the brick exterior of the house. The acolyte opened the van door and motioned me out as if to say, after you.

I rolled my eyes and scooted along the stretch of black carpet that lined the van's interior until I could swing my legs out the door and stand. I got up and brushed myself off, then opened my purse a smidgen and tossed my keys in before zipping it back up. They walked me to the front door, driver in front, acolyte in back. The driver knocked on the door three times in a slow rhythm, then a quick double knock. Good gods - these assholes even had a secret knock. This was every twelve-year-old boy's dream.

The door opened and I was pushed forward by Acolyte One. I stepped up into the house, into a living room straight out of nineteen-seventy-eight, full of green shag carpet and muted earth tones. The acolyte and driver didn't come in. They left. Literally left. I was alone with two men, the one holding the door and the one sitting on the couch. Benjamin Stone, AKA Drakaris Deathspell. I recognized him from the DMV photograph in the FBI file Stan had left with Mike.

"I don't know what you did to convince Maleficarus that you were possessed by the Daemon Lucifuge." He looked behind me to the other guy. Probably another nameless acolyte. "Sharon, was it?"

"Our meeting wasn't until later this week." I felt myself clutching my bag. Gods, I just realized my real ID was in there, along with my phone. If it started to ring… or what if they searched my bag? My stomach twisted in momentary panic.

"Yeah, well, I changed it to now. Why are you so insistent on wanting to meet me? What is it that you have that I would have any interest in whatsoever?" He narrowed his eyes and cocked his head to one side as if doing this would somehow reveal my motivation.

"I didn't even know your group existed until Maleficarus and I met at the coffee shop, and he started telling me about this badass Satanic coven he was in. I've been looking for a decent coven for some time, so I thought I'd inquire." It sounded so stupid as the words fell from my mouth, but I was already neck deep in it. There was no backing down now.

"You pretended to be possessed?" Drakaris looked at the guy behind me and laughed.

My stomach did a somersault. "Now, I don't remember that. I just remember…" A wave of relief washed over me as I felt that familiar sensation of the Daemon sliding into me, from my head and down into my body. But instead of taking over, Lucifuge just sat there, crouched inside me like a tiger waiting to pounce.

Drakaris raised an eyebrow.

"I black out sometimes," I said quickly, pausing to see if Lucifuge had anything to add. Nothing. I needed to explain, fast. "I don't remember most of our last meeting. I just black out. But I really am a Satanist looking for a coven, and according to Maleficarus, you're the real deal, in service of the Dark Lord himself. If you're legit, great. I want in."

"Define legit?" Drakaris seemed amused and patted the couch next to him.

You can jump in at any time, Lucifuge, I said inwardly.

You're doing great, Lucifuge answered in a life-coach kinda way. His response reminded me of my high school gym teacher who often shouted things like, *"keep going - it's hard!"* during burpees with a huge smile on her perfect, perky face. I'd always wanted to punch her and say, *you do a few of these damn burpees and tell us how hard it is, Miss J.*

I forced myself to sit next to Drakaris on the couch. "By legit, I mean you aren't just a bunch of boys looking to have orgies and pretend to be dark and scary? This isn't a social club for you? It's the real deal?"

Drakaris leaned into me and it took everything in my power not to lean completely back on the couch, but my back was rigid, the muscles so tense I could feel them tightening as if bracing for impact. His hot, cigarette breath hit me square in the face. "We are the real thing. Thank you for recognizing that. So, which part of our mission most interests you?"

My mind raced, scrambling for a good answer. "Any work our Dark Lord wishes us to do here on earth. Whatever that is, I'm in."

"Anything?" A slow grin slid over Drakaris' thin, dry lips.

Shit, I scolded myself. "Yes."

"Well, you'll have to prove your loyalty." He shared another glance with the man still standing by the door.

This is where they rape me, I immediately thought. Lucifuge remained silent. "Fine. What do you need? Steal some supplies? Recruit some more people? Or are we talking sexual favors because…"

He held up a hand. "Nothing like that. The high priestess isn't into sharing. Pity. But you will allow my colleague here to pat you down and check your purse. He's my security officer."

Dark Warlord Sethial, I thought. I was screwed now. They'd see my phone and my ID. I'd be made before the investigation began and Stan would be pissed when he learned I probably just blew months of investigation.

Don't panic, Lucifuge said in such a soothing way, that I literally felt the change in my body. I suddenly felt like I did in meditation: calm, relaxed, and even lighter somehow.

"Weird, but okay," I said, giving him an uncertain smile.

Sethial stepped forward and took my bag, opening it right there on the side arm of the couch and sifting through my things. He took out my phone and looked at it. He was scrolling through something. My social media? My contacts? Slowly the calm began to give way to panic again. Lucifuge gave me another shot of *calm.*

Then Sethial opened my wallet and sifted through it. Finally, he tossed the wallet back into the bag, then motioned me to stand. You would think being felt up by a strange man would have been a violation, but it was so mechanical and professional that it felt almost clinical. Sethial was all business.

"She's clean. No wires. ID and phone prove who she is. She doesn't have any social media on her phone and her only contacts are her boss." He walked back over to the side of the room to stand sentry again.

"Wires? Wait, are you guys doing illegal shit or something?" I narrowed my eyes. Knowing I might have overplayed the good-girl bit, I shrugged. "Well, if you are, I suppose it's the Dark Lord's will."

"You'll be witness to what the dark lord wants from his children. We will show you, and once you see, you'll be on board for everything. You'll be at twenty-third and Vance on Friday afternoon at two. You will be picked up by one of the acolytes and brought to our headquarters. There, you will meet the others and help us fulfill His work. We don't allow initiation into the inner sanctum until you've done some time doing the work though. Is that clear?"

His authoritative tone made my insides jump a little, and not in a good way. "Should I bring anything?"

"A week's worth of clothing. If in a week we don't think you're a good fit, we'll bring you back, and you can go back to your life," he said with a chilling grin.

Somehow, I knew that if Drakaris and Sethial didn't think I was a good fit, I wouldn't be coming home. Not alive anyway. A chill ran through me. "Sounds great." As I said it, an acrid taste filled my mouth, and suddenly I felt like I needed air.

I jumped when someone knocked on the door. Three knocks, then two fast.

"You're ride's here. We'll see you Friday, Sharon." Drakaris forced his grin wider.

There was something about that grin. For the life of me, after I left and climbed back into the van with the driver and acolyte, I couldn't remember Drakaris' face - only that grin.

I managed the long ride back to Parties Plus, where my car sat in the parking lot, unscathed. My bag was gone. I waited for the van to drive away before I got into my car, but then realized they knew my car and my license number. Lucifuge was still quietly along for the ride, but he didn't interject anything, maybe because things were getting serious, or maybe because he really had nothing to say. I wasn't sure, and he didn't provide insight.

Once I made it home and I was safely in the house, I checked my phone. Mike hadn't called back yet.

"Don't worry. I promise the wires will be undetectable," Stan said. He ran his hand over his receding hairline as if to shove imaginary hair from his face. We all sat at the dining room table, the surface scattered with paperwork from the case file.

Mike shot him a divisive look and let out a sigh. "I can't let her do this. They fucking kidnapped her in front of a store."

"Yeah - and she kept a cool head through it all and came out unharmed. We're going to get this guy..." He took out a notebook from his back pocket and began furiously scribbling in it. "We're going to have to use some in-clothing listening devices."

Mike threw his arms up. "If she's made - they kill her!"

They'd been going at this for fifteen minutes like I wasn't even in the room, because so far, not a single person had asked me how I felt about it.

Stan pointed to me. "She knows these people. She's good under pressure. We'll have agents surrounding the place. The second anything goes down, we're on them."

A deep frown scarred Mike's face and, finally, he looked at me, almost pleading.

"I can do this. We need to see what they're up to and take their operation out before they hurt a bunch of people," I said, marveling at how I sounded like an agent myself. I wanted to rush to him and wrap my arms around him and assure him everything would be okay, but I wasn't sure about that myself.

"I can't... I don't know. I..." He gave me a helpless look, one I wasn't accustomed to seeing, and it broke my heart.

"I have to do this or I'll never forgive myself if they succeed in hurting people." I let out a sigh and looked down at my feet, suddenly ashamed for wanting to help. Ashamed that I was willing to put myself in danger at the protests of the only man I'd ever loved.

"Fine, but I'm on the response team and I want a direct wire into everything as it goes down," Mike said, resolute. He crossed his arms over his chest and gave me that look that said we'd be having a discussion about it later.

But the discussion never came. The astral lessons stopped and Lucifuge had been strangely silent, so when Friday arrived, Mike held me in his arms that morning without a word. We both knew that Stan was right - I was the best person for the job to give them an inside look into what was going on inside the cult's compound. They armed me with an underwire bra, the underwire a listening device. Microphones in my coat, shoes, and on my belt buckle, and a pen that took pictures. They completed the ensemble with a temporary cell phone and fake ID, just in case Sethial decided to search my things again.

Armed with a backpack with a week's change of clothing, and a newly formed lump in my throat, they dropped me off at the pickup point fifteen minutes before I was supposed to be there. Then, we waited.

CHAPTER 10

Lucifuge showed up after the van arrived to collect me. It wasn't Maleficarus like I expected. Instead, I was picked up by the unnamed acolyte driver. Again, he did not offer his name.

You may not be prepared for what you are about to see, Lucifuge said. *It's not just the ideals or actions of this cult and its leader that are so dangerous.*

The winding road twisted around up the mountainside and, finally, the driver slowed and took a right turn onto a gravel access road. We started up the long winding road, the truck jostling us about. I held on to the *oh shit* bar and closed my eyes. I'd never been a fan of mountain driving just because I had a not-so-irrational fear of heights. With my eyes squeezed shut, I did not realize just how long we'd been driving before we pulled off into a driveway that led to a big house surrounded by trees. Two pillars flanked either side of the house and upon them stood two stone gargoyle statues. The statues scowled at us as the truck pulled to a stop and the driver turned off the ignition.

"Here we are," he said. "I think you'll really like it here."

It was doubtful. I felt the eyes of the two gargoyles watching me as I got out of the truck and reached into the back and pulled out Sharon's knapsack. The only things in my pack were a few pairs of jeans, a few shirts, some underwear, and some travel-size toiletries. The camera pen and a blank notebook were among my belongings. I wasn't expecting to stay very long and hoped Stan and crew could have it wrapped up in forty-eight hours. But Drakaris and his minions didn't know that. With my pack hefted over my shoulder, I turned toward the house and looked up at it. While it was made of brick, it still looked run down. Clearly whoever owned this place didn't see fit to do regular maintenance. The front door opened and two men in black, cowl-hooded robes stepped out, their faces shielded from us by the folds of the fabric.

"Brother," the taller one said to the driver. I recognized the voice as belonging to Drakaris. The fact that they lived out their fantasy in real life by wearing robes made me cackle on the inside. "I see you've brought us the new recruit." Then the man turned his attention on me. "Welcome. What will we call you here?"

I fought back an eye-roll. "Can't I just use my real name? Sharon. Sharon Smith." It was easiest just to keep it simple. Besides, Sharon Smith was a name I wouldn't easily forget, which was exactly why I'd chosen it. I forced a fake smile, hoping it wasn't too obvious.

"That won't do," Drakaris said. "How about Sister Sinestria?"

Proud that I was able to hold my tongue, I nodded in agreement. Lucifuge chuckled.

My mouth went dry as I glanced around again. There was something dark about this place. I know, I work with Daemons, and at the moment, I was possessed by Lucifuge. However, I could still feel... feel something. Divine Intelligences weren't heavy like this.

Seek with your mind, Lucifuge told me. *Then you will see what I see, and you will understand why I needed to bring you here and why I had you do all that work in the celestial temple.*

I drew in a deep breath, pretending to take in the mountain air even though what entered my lungs was heavy with something I couldn't quite place my finger on.

Death, Lucifuge said. *That's the word you're looking for.*

While it didn't smell like a death, Lucifuge was right. I'd sensed death energy before, but usually along with it came the sickening, sweet smell of rotting flesh. I focused and reached my mind out in every direction, the gooseflesh rising on my arms. From the corner of my right eye, I saw one of the gargoyles move. But that was impossible, stone didn't move, and Lucifuge told me that this cult, this doomsday cult, had no magical power of its own. So how could this be? I carefully turned my head, pretending to survey my surroundings, and that's when I saw it. It wasn't the gargoyle that was alive. There was something straddling it, and it was dark and vicious and hungry. I turned back to the robed men and forced another smile. "It really is beautiful up here."

The men were close enough now that I could see the lower half of their faces. Drakaris said, "We find it suits our needs for privacy. Come, let Sethial show you to the room that you'll be sharing with several other women. Our quarters are not elaborate, but they suffice. They help us do the work that we must do, and that is all that matters."

Cautiously, I approached the steps and ascended to the porch, thankful that it wasn't as rickety as it looked. Sethial sprinted ahead of me and opened the door, ushering me inside. I had to force my legs to move past the threshold, that thick and heavy death energy setting every instinct I had on edge. If it weren't for Lucifuge keeping me balanced and steady, I would have bolted like a frightened horse. I kept forcing myself to smile, feeling the muscles in my cheeks hurt. Perhaps it was a sign I didn't smile enough, or perhaps it was a sign of how tense I actually was. *Lucifuge?* I asked inwardly. *Please tell me you're here.*

I know this is hard, he said. *Don't worry, I'm with you.*

These words gave me the strength I needed to move further into the common living area of the house. It was dark and there were old tattered sheets covering the windows. Piles of books and papers lay everywhere, littering the floor. The dark blue furniture, covered in stains and old blankets, looked like it had seen better days. The entire place smelled like an animal den. It was obvious the cult's priorities did not include cleaning, and while I wasn't much of a housekeeper myself, being here made me want to find a broom and vacuum and get to work. Though that wasn't the only type of cleaning this place needed.

Exactly, Lucifuge said. *We're standing almost on top of an open portal.*

"Are the others here?" I asked, trying to muster some enthusiasm.

Sethial, with his hands folded in front of him, shook his head. "No. They are all out back, working on our mission. Come, let me show you upstairs."

I followed the robed man to the staircase and up the creaking stairs.

Now look at the back of his neck, Lucifuge said.

I reached out with my mind, focusing on the back of Sethial's neck and stopped short on the staircase. The thick, black, semi-opaque mass undulated against Sethial's skin like an earthworm wriggling into a hole. How come I hadn't noticed it before?

Keep moving, don't let on to knowing what's actually going on. If they think you know, we might have a problem, Lucifuge said. *They're easier to see when you're on top of the portal. Down in the city, they almost vanish. This is the place of their power.*

I drew up all my strength and began moving again, quickening my pace so I could catch back up. What I saw on the back of brother Sethial's neck gave me the willies. There was some sort of dark energy creature attached to him.

That, Lucifuge said, *is what you call an Other. It's a vile, feeder spirit from the open portal in this place.*

You don't actually expect me to take one of those on just to be here, I said inwardly to Lucifuge, shocked at the idea that he would expect me to host a feeder spirit just to take down a doomsday cult.

I will simulate it to make them think you've been taken over, so that we don't arouse suspicion when we do the exorcism and close the portal.

Heavy realization smacked me upside the head. *So, we're not here to take out the bombs and foil their plans for murdering hundreds if not thousands of people?*

Lucifuge's voice turned solemn. *No. Your job is to help me exorcize the spirits and close this portal before it grows too large and opens a rift to a different sphere. Rifts are harder to close than portals. It is Michael and Stan's job to deal with the bombs and to foil the murders of thousands.*

Brother Sethial, or Dark Warlord Sethial according to the email the BMN had received, led me into a medium sized room with two bunk beds. "Here we are. You will be sharing this room with Sister V, Sister Y, and Sister C. If they choose to tell you their chosen names, that's fine. You are welcome to use Sister S. It suits you. It appears that you have the bunk on the lower right side." He motioned toward the bunk that looked freshly made and uncluttered with personal belongings.

I found myself relieved that I wouldn't have to sleep on the top bunk and that the room looked well-kept. At least my roommates weren't messy. There was a single writing desk on the same wall as the doorway, and a small en suite bathroom next to a sizable, but packed, walk-in closet. Near the window stood a vase of flowers, but they were dead. The energy suckers had probably stolen the life from them too.

"I'll leave you to freshen up and then I will give you a tour of the rest of the house. You will not be allowed into the inner sanctum until after your trial period and initiation," Brother Sethial said. Then he turned and left, pulling the door partially closed behind him. I heard his footfalls move through the hallway and back to the staircase, then down. I could tell I was the only person on the second floor now, but the air around me writhed with the nasty energy.

Not nasty energy, Lucifuge said. *What you feel are the entities writhing around you like snakes, they're checking you out. Sniffing you to find your weaknesses.*

Fear twisted my stomach. "But you won't let them take me," I said, just to be sure.

No, Lucifuge said inwardly. *The initiation ceremony is when they attach the creature to you if one doesn't attach itself of its own accord. As I said, I will simulate one of the creatures myself and will take over your body. They will think I am one of them. Being able to walk among them is of utmost importance if we are going to be able to do this.*

"But I don't have any ritual tools," I whispered, immediately realizing how stupid that was. Lucifuge had been pushing me to do astral work for weeks now. This was why. Tools weren't necessary. Then I remembered I was covered in microphones and realized how ridiculous that must have sounded.

Don't speak aloud, we might be overheard. Listen, he said. *You have me and that is all we will need. We just need to find where the portal is and then find the right time to close it. We will have to figure that out as we go along.*

Can't you see the future? I thought.

Lucifuge chuckled, but it was strained. *Time is not linear, but that aside - the future is not set. I can see several possible outcomes.*

It was a typical cryptic response. While I hated it when Daemons weren't direct, I knew that Lucifuge wasn't telling me the whole truth for a reason. If I'd learned anything from several decades of practice working with the Daemonic, it was that I trusted them, and they never lied to me.

I slung my pack from my shoulder and threw it onto the bed, then sat down heavily, careful not to hit my head on the top bunk. I examined the underside of the bunk above me to make sure it was sturdy and that there were no spiders. This was not an ideal situation, but it had to be done. With a sigh, I heaved myself up out of the bed and checked out the closet and the bathroom. Both were relatively neat and tidy, and I could tell the bathroom had been recently cleaned. Even with those things attached to them, the women still had enough energy to clean, which I took as a good sign. Maybe it meant that they'd only been recently attached to the creatures, or rather entities. Perhaps that meant it would be easier to detach the entities as well. Of course, if I knew anything about spirits, I knew they wouldn't go down without a fight, and secretly I hoped that Lucifuge and I were enough to exorcize the whole lot of them and send them back through the portal from whence they came. Then, we'd have to slam it shut as quickly as possible so none of them remained. Suddenly, the task felt overwhelming.

One step at a time, Lucifuge said. *Don't panic on me, Elizabeth.*

Why couldn't you just come here by yourself? Why did you need me? To me, the Daemonic was all-powerful, and I couldn't understand why the Daemonic couldn't just banish these things from this world themselves. They were certainly strong enough.

It's much easier to do while anchored to the earth sphere. That means having a human host to deal with the problem. Allowing this portal to stay open and rip into a large rift could plummet this world into darkness and throw the rest of the spheres into chaos. We are the balance in chaos, and we are stewards to the physical realm. I felt Lucifuge settle into the base of my neck. *Now let's get down there before they start to have suspicions about what's taking you so long.*

With a nod, I quickly checked myself in the mirror and then made my way back downstairs. I found the driver and the two robed men in the kitchen, drinking steaming mugs of tea. I found that almost laughable, considering the two robed men both had the dark entities attached to them. The driver did not for some reason, and I wondered why. Was it because he needed energy to go out and recruit new people? That was a mystery I figured I'd solve once I gathered more information about how the coven operated.

The kitchen itself wasn't too terrible. The counters could've used some wiping down, and there were unwashed dishes in the sink, but there was a dishwasher and by the looks of it, a clean load of dishes inside.

Brother Sethial motioned me toward a chair at the large dining room table that sat eight. "Would you like some tea?"

I almost laughed because it was so ridiculous. "Yes, please."

There was a fourth mug, empty, on the table next to the teapot. Drakaris poured me a cup and pushed it toward me as I sat.

"I hope you found your quarters suitable?" Drakaris asked.

I nodded. "Quite. Thank you."

"Just last night, Maleficarus was telling us that you, Sister Sinestria, are quite the devoted Satanist." He motioned toward the sigil of Lucifuge tattoo that Lucifuge had placed on me during my first meeting with Maleficarus. It looked real enough, and I was still hoping it wasn't permanent even though I knew better. Lucifuge was good at changing my appearance to suit his needs.

It's only an illusion, Lucifuge had assured me.

I pulled the steaming mug of tea closer to me and gave Drakaris a nod. "I've been working with our Dark Lord, Satan, for a decade now." I held back a smile that always came when I said ridiculous phrases like *Dark Lord*. Of course, I wasn't opposed to Satanists, considering my best friend was the happiest Satanist on planet Earth. But Alyssa, while she was a Satanist, also understood that Satan was a title meaning Adversary and not an actual name. Alyssa was dedicated to gnosis, and while she did believe there was a sentient power behind the universe, she tried not to speculate what that was. She simply called it Satan, adversarial to the common religious culture. She believed in other spirits as well, including the Divine Intelligences, a.k.a. Daemons, but for her Satan, the adversarial knowledge, was a part of the whole of divinity. Or at least that's how I understood her beliefs to work. It was nothing like these people, though. These Satanists were theistic and believed in Satan and Daemons in the Christian sense. Satan and his Daemons were evil spirits bent on taking over the world and destroying all of mankind. And the Anti-Christ's Temple, their Dark Diocese, had every intention of helping their imaginary Devils do this.

But their Devils weren't imaginary. No, they were negative energy feeders streaming in from an open portal, demanding their own dominion, and ours. The world had a plentiful supply of energy, negative energy, that they could feed off of for some time, I imagined, and if that portal cracked open into a rift, that was a problem. I wondered then, albeit briefly, what a world full of humans hosting negative energy feeders, nasty spirits, would look like. One phrase popped into my mind – the zombie apocalypse. Though Sethial and Drakaris did seem rather cognizant, I imagined they probably didn't feel very good with those things leeching off of them. I still wondered how the driver had gotten away with not hosting one of his own.

"And what does the Lord Satan say to you?" Drakaris gave me an expectant look, and I felt my stomach sink.

I hadn't rehearsed any answers and I found myself struggling to answer now. I opened my mouth to say something, but it wasn't me who spoke. Lucifuge jumped in just in the nick of time. "Satan is the King of this world and it is under His dominion. It is by His word what will remain and what will be destroyed. I have every intention of following His orders."

This response seemed to satiate the three men. Drakaris grasped me on the shoulder and said, "Perhaps Maleficarus was right even if you did fool him. You are one of the chosen. I see it in your eyes. They flashed a blaze of red when you said that."

Sethial nodded. "You agree to host one of Satan's Daemons, then?"

Lucifuge hadn't left and said, "I'm quite willing. I am pleased to be among my own kind to serve our great King."

I reeled backward in my own mind, overwhelmed with how melodramatic it all was. It was almost as if these people were playing characters, living in their own fantasy world where their Christian sensibilities insisted that Satan was this evil being hell-bent on destroying mankind. Of course, that's probably what their controlling spirits had told them. Others, the negative feeders, had a bad habit of lying and pretending to be something they weren't.

As if he wanted to be sure, Drakaris narrowed his eyes at me. "You won't mind then if we do a divination to ensure that you are truly open to the Master?"

"I have no issue with that whatsoever," Lucifuge said.

The certainty in his voice caused Sethial to widen his eyes slightly and give me a pleasant smile. "Perhaps I should take you out now so you can meet the others."

Drakaris gave an approving nod and went back to his tea, while Lucifuge nodded my head and pushed the tea away without touching it.

I think this was the first time I'd ever seen Lucifuge push tea aside. Usually, he was intent on trying everything that the physical world had to offer. I was only thankful that he hadn't possessed me while Mike and I were having sex. That would've been awkward. I stifled a giggle inside my own mind until control of my limbs drifted away as Lucifuge pushed further into me and took over every part of my body. We stood and I followed Sethial from the kitchen.

The house was relatively good-sized, with five bedrooms upstairs and three bathrooms, and three bedrooms and one bathroom in the basement. The main floor housed the large living area, a dining room, and a large eat-in kitchen. On the back of the house was another veranda like the one out front, with stairs leading down to a stone pathway that led to a large outbuilding in the back. The entire property was surrounded with conifers and aspens and other pine trees. It was extremely remote, and for good reason. A doomsday cult wouldn't have wanted their neighbors peeking in on them to see what they were doing. When we reach the outbuilding, Sethial opened the door and held it for me, motioning me in.

The lights were on and I could hear people talking around the corner. We stepped in and I allowed Sethial to get ahead of me, or rather Lucifuge did, and he led me into a clearing where at least fifteen people sat around several long worktables, intently focused on whatever it was they were doing. It was a good thing Lucifuge had control of my faculties because when I saw the homemade bombs spread before them, I gasped inwardly. I wasn't sure I would've been able to hide that reaction, but Lucifuge did it perfectly and said, "You've all been quite busy. Are we ahead of schedule?"

Sethial took down his hood. For the first time, I really noticed that his hair was buzzed, and he had wild green eyes. In a way, he looked like a crazy man. Why hadn't I noticed this before? "This is Sister S., our newest recruit. She has yet to take on a Daemonic host, but she's willing."

I half expected one of them to shout out, *no wait, she's not legit.* I didn't have to wait long for an interesting response.

A tall, slender young woman, with a riot of brown, curly hair, contorted her fine features and said, "How come she's not hosting a Daemon now? I was hosting when I got here."

"That is for Satan to know and for us to learn," Sethial said, instantly silencing her. It was clear Sethial and Drakaris had a firm hand on their flock of sheep who seemed more than willing to bow down to their masters, likely to their own deaths. Even if they made it out alive with their subtle bodies intact, the entire lot of them would be heading to prison.

I only hoped that we would be able to exorcize the spirits and close the portal long before Mike, the FBI, and local law enforcement were able to get in here and shut this down. There were a few among Stan's crew that didn't care for an untrained civilian being used as a plant, but they had no choice, and I'd assured them all before they dropped me at the pickup that there was no way I'd let the bombs leave the building. If they did, innocent people would die. While this was the base of operation in the inner circle, there had to be more people involved than just these few.

A few of the men smiled at me, looking me up and down in that creepy lustful way that made me want to take a hot shower to sear my skin off. I certainly hoped they didn't think I was going to sleep with any of them. The thought of that made my insides shudder.

Lucifuge chuckled. *Not a chance,* he told me silently. At least he had my back. I'd seen how strong he was, even in my body. He'd helped me pick up a woman at least twice my size and hurl her across the room. Possessed by Lucifuge, I was a force to be reckoned with despite my short stature and medium build. I'd never been a skinny girl. Athletic was more like it, with curves. But I was in good shape and took care of myself, probably another reason Lucifuge had chosen me.

I felt a hand behind me. "Excuse me," came a familiar female voice. I froze. When I turned my head, there was Kara Jarvis, my recently fired assistant. The manipulative crybaby herself. *Wiccan, my ass.* But for some reason, by the powers of Lucifuge, she didn't recognize me and gave me a bright smile before taking her place at one of the bomb tables.

CHAPTER 11

Most of the members appeared to be in their twenties, which made me a bit self-conscious, considering I was a bit closer to the age of their two leaders.

Drakaris looked to be in his early thirties, though according to his file he was nearly forty. We all lingered in the kitchen while two of the women ladled soup from a large pot into mismatched bowls. From the big cans and bulk pasta I'd seen in the pantry cupboards, my guess was they shopped at a warehouse store and ate a lot of pasta and soup, and little else. Of course, that was the cheapest route to go when you had so many mouths to feed. Inwardly, I applauded their budgeting skills.

I'd been careful to avoid Kara at all costs just in case Lucifuge's glamour faltered. Navigating the coven was easier than I imagined, though tiresome. While I was used to people referring to Satan as *The Dark Lord*, phrases like *The Dark King* and *Master* seemed forced and melodramatic. It was almost over the top for me. They reminded me of Evangelists who had to bring their god into every conversation.

It was when a young blond woman said, "In Satan's name, this soup is delicious," and at least four people responded with, "In the name of Satan, Ruler of the earth, King of this world,

Praise be," that I almost lost it. I swear those were the lyrics to some metal song I'd recently heard.

Lucifuge interrupted my thoughts, and I could tell by his vibration that it was urgent. *I think we should try the first portal closing ritual tonight.*

I felt my face contort as I answered him in my mind. *But I just learned how to put together a bomb. You're ruining my fun.*

His reaction almost sent me into laughter. What felt like a groan rippled through me, and I was sure he was somehow rolling his astral eyes at me.

Just kidding, I thought. In my mind, I'd been going over the portal closing rituals I'd learned during my time as an apprentice, back when the occult world still had apprentice-teacher relationships. I had been incredibly lucky to have been one of the few magicians of my generation to have been taught by a real flesh and blood teacher. Nowadays, everyone learned from books or Internet searches. Everyone was an expert by the mere fact that they could use a search engine and knew how to read - or by listening to a streaming song by any random Satanic metal band.

I managed to keep to myself at the end of the table, listening to Sethial tell stories about his medieval reenactment group and the fake sword fights he won by playing a fake character on the weekend. I kept my head down and my mouth shut, only smiling or laughing when others did, just to fit in. It seemed fitting that one of the leaders acted out his knighthood fantasies in a make-believe feudal system.

Based on the email I'd seen that he or Drakaris had sent to the Black Magick Network, this cult - these Satanists - were just an extension of a masculine fantasy that permeated their waking moments. The things attached to them weren't making them do this - no, this was them. Pure human desire and imagination.

After what seemed too long, dinner finally ended, and we all moved to the living room. Drakaris and Kara took the couch and there, Kara cleared off the second-hand coffee table, its surface marred with deep scratches and discoloration from drinking glasses left far too long. From the black bag she'd brought with her, she pulled out *The Black Deck* based on what it said on the box, a tarot deck that I assumed was strictly for those who practiced the dark arts. With a snap and a whir, she shuffled the cards, silencing everyone in the room. Then with great concentration, she laid the cards out in the pattern of an inverse pentacle.

"Isn't that the spread for the Black Meditation?" One of the men asked reverently, eyes wide, as if it was a sacred thing.

I'd never heard of such a thing and bit my inner cheek. The entire coven held its breath as she looked over the cards one by one. Shit, this was it. She was going to reveal me. My heart pounded.

Relax, she doesn't even recognize you. I'm very good at glamors, Lucifuge said, that calming effect washing over me like a wave. *Breathe.*

I closed my eyes and drew in a breath. When I opened my eyes, I was relieved to find no one was looking at me. All eyes were fixed on Kara, the coven seer. I glanced toward the front door. Six or seven wide strides, and I could reach it and make my escape. The sprint to the main road would be tough, but it was downhill at least. In my imaginary escape attempt, Mike and the FBI would be waiting on the main road. My escape fantasy didn't include the two men who currently stood between me and the door. One of them could easily grab me and keep me from freedom.

Don't lose your nerve now! Lucifuge's voice had an edge to it. I straightened and turned my attention back to Kara.

"A time of great awakening is upon us," she announced with a smile.

Murmurs of relief and affirmation swept through the group.

"The Dark Lord smiles upon us, and we are blessed!" She gave him a wide, eerie grin and turned to look at Drakaris.

He responded with a nod of approval. "Brothers and sisters, let's raise a glass to Satan!" Then he nodded to a young, portly man with wire-rim glasses, and the man went to a tall cupboard and opened it, revealing a hidden mini bar.

The acolyte took up a bottle of Jack Daniels. "Jack all around?"

A resounding yes moved through the room.

You can't have any of that. We need to do the astral ritual, Lucifuge said. *Let's try to break away.*

Lucifuge was right. At this altitude, the whiskey would go straight to my head, and there would be no way I'd be able to do a ritual, let alone much else. All the same, I needed to wait a little longer, pretend to be part of the group.

When a glass of whiskey was offered to me, I smiled politely. "No, thank you. It upsets my stomach."

"Lightweight, huh?" the guy beside me asked.

I shook my head. "I have a little altitude sickness is all. It's been a long day."

He accepted this and moved on to click glasses with some of the people next to him and everyone drank.

I shrank back into the background. The longer I sat in that room, the more anxious I became. Was the FBI picking up any of this? They hadn't swooped in, so apparently, I hadn't gotten them what they needed. Was Mike worried about me? Were the wires even working? Was the boredom of this droll party putting those in the listening van to sleep? I mostly kept to the corner by a table of dust-covered, fake plants, smiled, and nodded, and said *Hail Satan* when appropriate. Alyssa probably would have told me it was always appropriate to say *Hail Satan*, especially if those prone to pearl-clutching were within earshot.

Every stereotypical Satanist in every bad Hollywood movie was embodied in this small group of practitioners. Luckily, none of them seemed overly concerned enough to force me to participate. After about twenty minutes blending with the wall and plants, I made my move toward the stairs, hoping to slip away before anyone noticed.

Sethial stepped in front of me right when I thought I was going to get away with it. "Calling it an early night?" He looked concerned. "You should stay and socialize."

I stalled for a moment but found my voice. "The excitement of the day, and this altitude, it really wore me out. I'm so tired." I gave him a weak smile and tried to force my eyes and body to droop, if such a thing was possible.

Good, Lucifuge said in the back of my mind. *They might think the bonding is happening. Then you won't have to worry about them not accepting you, but we'll deal with that more completely tomorrow if we cannot close the portal tonight.*

Oh joy, I thought. I gave Sethial another smile, broader this time, more forced. If I knew anything, I knew that if you wanted to influence people, Satanists or not, you complimented them. "Thank you for everything, Brother Sethial."

He patted my arm like a concerned father. "Yes, get some sleep. You'll have a full day tomorrow, and if all goes well, tomorrow night you'll be able to attend Black Rite."

"Good night." I managed another weak smile and started up the stairs, my mind racing, wondering what the fuck Black Rite was, and leaving behind the cacophony of voices below as I ascended to the cool darkness of the second floor. Lucifuge had stayed with me all afternoon and evening. He lounged inside me, casually hanging back and watching everything I did. The constant reminder that I wasn't alone comforted me. I could feel Lucifuge so acutely that it made me wonder if the members of the coven felt their feeders. Was there pressure on their necks where the things were attached? Or were the majority of them so psychically inept that they were blind to it? For those who did feel it, did they notice their energy and willpower slowly slipping away? Did they fight it?

Amid the wondering, I changed my clothes and put on black sweatpants and a gray tank top, perfectly acceptable ritual attire for working in the astral. Then I slipped between the cool sheets of the bottom bunk that was mine and picked up my shoe, finding the microphone.

I listened carefully for any noise beyond the closed bedroom door, before whispering into my shoe, "So, here's the deal, you guys - the bombs are in the garage out back. They have about fifty assembled so far, but you said I needed to get someone to talk about bombs and the plan openly so you could record it. I couldn't get pictures because there were too many people around. Unfortunately, these people are all, *Satan's work this and Satan's work that*. I'm working on it. I'll start again tomorrow because I'm damn tired. Tell Mike I said goodnight. I hope you can hear me."

It was frustrating not being able to have a two-way conversation. All I knew is I was supposed to get one of these people to confess a plan in plain English, without all the archaic references to *The Dark Lord's plan*. I was supposed to get pictures as proof of a bomb. Both tasks were easier said than done.

I drew in a deep breath and closed my eyes.

You're going to fall asleep, Lucifuge cautioned.

I am not, I thought. *I'm going to go to my celestial temple, and we're doing this ritual.*

Lucifuge groaned.

I started my ascension to the astral and made it into the temple before drifting off to sleep and dreaming of nothing.

CHAPTER 12

You fell asleep! Lucifuge was clearly upset.

My eyes flew open, and I looked around, half expecting to find the Daemon leaning over me with a scowl on his face. *Sorry,* I thought. *I didn't mean to, I was exhausted.*

We have to do it tonight, no exceptions, he said with a hint of finality to his voice.

Okay, I answered inwardly. *Maybe we can do it today. I'll go take a walk and we can find a good spot.*

Fine, Lucifuge said.

I don't know when the others had finally come to bed, only that they were there now, sleeping soundly, snuggled under their blankets against the chill of the frigid mountain air. Worried about waking them, I planned my exit. I slipped out of bed, grabbed my sweatshirt and jacket, took my shoes from under the bed, and tip-toed out of the room and down the stairs in stocking feet. The first hints of light beamed through the windows, making it easy to navigate my way through the house. I needed to get out of here. I found my way to the empty kitchen, wondering if Mike and Stan were still listening, or if the equipment was even working. I thought about whispering a snarky comment into the wired tennis shoes that

I held against my chest but thought better of it. I couldn't risk someone walking in only to find me talking to my shoes. The bulky sweatshirt was also wired. Somewhere in the thick fabric, they'd found a way stitch in listening devices and a GPS tracker. I felt like James Bond.

Slipping on my shoes, I went out onto the back porch. The heavy energy didn't dissipate, even outside. It was always there, covering the entire area in and around the house with thick and writhing sludge that pressed against me. The air I breathed into my lungs should have been light, crisp and cold, but instead it was soggy and suffocating.

Relax, Lucifuge told me. His insistence that I relax was becoming more common, it seemed. Then, around me, there was a pop, and the air suddenly turned lighter, and I could breathe again. I drew in a deep breath of the crisp morning, no longer struggling to inhale.

Thank you, I told him inwardly. Even then I knew it was only a temporary fix, and I didn't want Lucifuge wasting all of his energy on helping me feel more comfortable when we had bigger issues. The coven was meddling with things they didn't understand and had unleashed a force more dangerous than a hundred bombs. If I was struggling to breathe in the presence of an open rift, I could only imagine the effect it was having on the plants and animals. Suddenly, it fully dawned on me why Lucifuge was so insistent and worried.

I knew there was no way I was going to get into the barn to take pictures. It was too suspicious. That's when I decided I needed a better idea of how big this portal was so that, when Lucifuge and I did the ritual to close it, I'd know how far to extend my own light in order to seal it. That meant taking a walk - not only to clear my head and get more air, but to see the bigger picture. The first rays of actual sunlight began to break on the horizon, and I could almost feel the thick frost that covered everything starting to melt. Shoving my hands into my pockets, I stepped down from the porch and began walking toward the forest. I needed a better vantage point, and I saw one about a mile up the mountain that looked good. Just as my FBI wired tennis shoes hit the trail leading up, I heard a woman's voice from behind me.

"Sister S, where are you going?"

I turned and found myself face to face with Drakaris' girlfriend who referred to herself only as Sister Y. She was friends with another woman at the compound who called herself Sister C and, of course, she was a friend to Kara - my mewling former office assistant. "I was going to take a walk up the mountain a ways." I forced a grin.

She was dressed in black yoga pants and a black tank top trimmed with lace. Over that, she wore a blue zip-up hoodie. On her feet, she sported a pair of black cross trainers. Her eyes followed mine up the mountain.

"Do you want to come?" I asked. I didn't want to appear suspicious, and not inviting her would have seemed odd.

"Okay, but maybe we should tell someone, tell the others..." She anxiously looked back at the still slumbering house, nervously fidgeting with the shoelace ties of her hoodie.

I looked at the house, too, and shrugged. "No sense in waking them up. They're still sleeping. We'll be back by the time they're all rolling out of bed for their coffee," I assured her. "What are you doing up so early?"

"Yoga." There was still hesitation in her voice.

"Looks like we're both early risers. I like to walk or go for a jog first thing in the morning. It gets me ready for my day. Let's go." I forced another grin.

She cringed.

"Look, I am pretty sure Satan wouldn't object to two of his dedicants maintaining physically fit bodies to host the Daemonic," I said. "We have to stay strong to do his work."

That was all it took. Her expression softened with relief, and for the first time since I arrived the day before, Sister Y gave me a genuine smile. "Okay."

We started walking. She stayed behind me, every so often looking back as if taking a simple walk was a violation of coven protocol. Lucifuge hadn't chimed in, but I could feel him, prone inside my consciousness, watching and listening. His presence comforted me. We followed the winding path, gently sloping upward, between the conifers and pine, and made our way up the trail. All the while, I purposefully ignored the ugly black ball of energy firmly attached to the back of Sister Y's neck. Even when I wasn't looking at it, I could still feel the creature's presence behind me, like a dark spot of nastiness smudged across the landscape.

We walked in silence for a while until the quiet became deafening. It was almost as uncomfortable as the energy around us. It seemed odd not to hear birds, and I wondered if she noticed it, too. I decided not to ask.

"How long have you and Drakaris been friends?" It seemed a natural segue into a conversation.

She lengthened her stride until she was walking beside me and slowed again to meet my shorter gait. "I've known him for two years now. We met at The Chapel."

The Chapel was a local goth hangout in Denver, and it didn't surprise me that Drakaris frequented the place. A lot of local practitioners, especially older men looking for young girlfriends, hung out there. It was one of the reasons I never had. "Cool," I said, not really knowing how to elaborate on that.

"You?" The pitch in her voice told me she really didn't know anything about me, or how I came to be part of their little group. Sethial and Drakaris hadn't told anyone the circumstances of my involvement. For that, I was grateful because it would make things easier.

"We met through a mutual friend not too long ago. I had a hell of a time convincing my friend to introduce us. Finding a legit Satanic coven is hard, you know?" I gave her just enough truth to keep it from sounding awkward. Besides, she didn't need to know that Maleficarus and I weren't actual friends. Maybe acquaintances at best. I examined the trees as we passed them, and dread began forming in the pit of my stomach. Many of the pines' needles appeared to be turning brown at the tips of their branches, losing their deep green color. That couldn't be good because, if my gut was right, it meant the rift was starting to kill the forest.

"Yeah, true." The pitch in her voice rose again and excitement lit up her eyes. "Drakaris is the Dark Lord's chosen priest. He doesn't just let anyone into the coven. We're the chosen servants of Satan."

She really believed that. I hurried to manufacture some enthusiasm. "I am so excited that Drakaris allowed me to come. I was worried for a bit, but I don't blame him. There are a lot of poseurs out there who want to claim to be servants of the Master, but when it comes down to it, they don't want to do what He asks of them."

She nodded emphatically. "I know, right?" Then she stopped dead in her tracks and cocked her head to one side. "Have you been chosen to carry a Daemon yet?"

A quiver of nausea ran through me. "Not yet. I mean, I can feel them all around me, checking me out, but I haven't gotten one. Is that normal?"

She started walking again. "It happens differently for everyone. Most of us are claimed by a Daemonic companion within the first few days we're here. Some people need more help, and Drakaris has to do the bonding ritual during the initiation." Then her mood went dark. "If that fails, they can't be initiated into the coven."

The way she said that sent a chill up my spine. Lucifuge immediately jumped in. *They've killed several strong-willed individuals who fought the bonding of the feeder spirit. They can't risk anyone knowing about their operation.*

How do they justify the killing to their followers? This woman isn't a murderer. I can feel it. I've met murderers before…

Lucifuge washed that calming energy over me. *They tell them Satan has demanded a sacrifice. If you aren't one of the chosen, you're a lamb fit for the slaughter.*

And if you weren't here and they tried to attach one of those things to me? I watched the Daemons expression in my mind's eye.

You are too damn stubborn. You'd be a sacrifice, but you don't have to worry. I have a plan. Lucifuge gave me a mental smirk, and I could almost feel the glint in his eye.

"What happens if someone isn't chosen by a Daemonic companion?" I asked her carefully. I wanted to see if she would tell me the truth of it.

She didn't. "They have to serve Satan in another way. They're not one of the chosen."

"Aren't you guys worried those who aren't chosen are going to feel rejected and talk shit about you online or something?" Yes, I was poking the bear, but it seemed to amuse the Daemon within.

"Yeah, probably. Drakaris deals with all of that." When she lied, she twisted her jaw to the right ever so slightly and looked away. I filed that information away for later.

We were almost to the high point I had my sights on, and I noticed it was getting easier to breathe and the creatures' energy seemed to be thinning. *Almost there*, I thought. Then I glanced at Sister Y, wondering if the *Other* on her neck would be able to survive outside her environment. As we got closer and closer, the air cleared even more, and I felt my legs carrying me faster. I felt like I could run now, and if I wanted, Sister Y and I could have gotten away into the forest and never looked back. Even the trees were greener here, and for the first time that morning, I heard birds singing. When we finally reached the lookout point, tears stung my eyes, and if I could have, I would have fallen to my knees, sobbing.

Hands on my hips, I looked out over the surrounding area. It looked just like any beautiful mountain vista, but when I opened my third eye and looked harder, I saw it for what it was.

I felt Sister Y touch my arm. "Are you okay? Why are you crying?"

For the first time, I felt the tears streaming down my cheeks. I'd thought I'd been able to hold in my relief to be out of the murk, but my subconscious had other ideas. "Sorry." I wiped my eyes. "It's just so beautiful up here. It moves me."

Lucifuge chuckled.

Which made me laugh outwardly and made Sister Y draw back in confusion. I shook my head, "Sorry. I just realized how ridiculous I must look right now. I can get so emotional sometimes, for stupid reasons."

She nodded. "I understand." Then she looked out over the valley below with me. "It is really pretty."

Sister Y didn't see what I now saw. She didn't know about the nasty thing on her neck, sucking away her life force. No, breaching the barrier didn't cause it to lose hold. But worse, in front of me, a long scar about two miles long and a mile wide marred the valley below, and it was growing.

Fuck, I said inwardly.

Yeah, Lucifuge agreed.

Wouldn't it be easier to close from up here? I wondered. *I could do it right here.*

I think you have to be at its origination point to do it properly. We should do it soon. It wasn't this big yesterday, the Daemon said with conviction. *It was only about three quarters the size of this. If it's growing a quarter to half a mile each day, or even every twelve hours, we can't wait. We have to do the ritual sometime today or tonight. It will be a mile longer and a half mile wider. We should have done it last night.*

Sorry, I thought again. *I was tired.*

Yes, I know. I often forget the limitations of the physical body, and I'm sorry to have been so hard on you. Then the Daemon pointed out approximations of that distance to me, so I had a clear visual to work with. I focused, trying to sear it into my brain.

Sister Y was patient, but she clearly wasn't one to meditate because, after about ten minutes, she started fidgeting again. "We should probably get back."

"I just want to remember this moment," I said, taking another deep breath and knowing it was the last clean air I'd have for another twenty hours or so.

I want you to drop to your knees now, cry out, and stare ahead like you're having some kind of seizure, Lucifuge said, his voice urgent.

It must have been the tone in which he relayed this message because it sent horror through me as if I'd seen something terrifying, and I followed his order without question, dropping to my knees and not even flinching when a rock tore into my jeans and bit into my right knee-cap. That was going to leave a bruise. I opened my eyes wide and stared straight ahead, forcing my body to shake a little. Fully committed to acting out whatever this was.

You're getting your guardian Daemon – they just won't know it's me, Lucifuge said.

Good thing, too. Though did you ever consider that maybe if you just possessed me and told them who you were and why we needed to close the portal that they would comply? It was such a simple plan, and yet here we were.

The feeders would have convinced them that I was lying. The feeders control their will. They really do believe the feeders are Daemons. It's too bad they don't know what Daemons are exactly, he said. I could tell their perception of the Daemonic left Lucifuge feeling disgusted. It dripped from every word.

I stopped convulsing and stared straight ahead, eyes wide, then began gasping for air. Sister Y knelt down next to me and took me by the elbow, helping me up. A heavy weight sat on the back of my neck and between my shoulder blades. It was Lucifuge, squatting in the same spot the feeders favored. I was now, technically, possessed.

Sister Y smiled at me. It was as if she sensed I had changed somehow. Not in the way she thought, but in the way Lucifuge and I wanted her to think. "Are you okay?"

I nodded uncertainly. "I feel a little light-headed. I don't know what happened."

"It's okay," she chirped, pleased as punch. "You've just gone through the metamorphosis. It's different for everyone, but you've been chosen!"

Then she hugged me, and it took every ounce of willpower I had to avoid stiffening and flinching away. "How do you know?"

"My guardian Daemon told me, silly," she said, drawing back and beaming at me, her teeth white and perfect and eyes blue and clear. "This is great news. We should go tell Drakaris immediately!"

I smiled back at her, the muscles in my cheeks burning with fatigue. "Okay, yes, let's tell him."

We have to be very careful now. We have to convince them that you are possessed by a spirit they think is Daemonic, but we also have to convince the other spirits that I'm one of them. Otherwise, they might turn the coven against us. Lucifuge went silent then.

I could feel Lucifuge's concern in his tone. The game we were playing dealt with a delicate balance where, if one scale was tipped too far in the wrong direction, I was in danger of death, and Lucifuge would not be able to close the portal. A portal that would grow out of control and potentially wipe out an already fragile planet.

Sister Y took my hand and practically dragged me toward the trail leading back to the house. "Come on."

She was really excited. Then I remembered my second mission. I needed to get their plan, the sooner, the better. If I could get the information, the FBI could close in, removing the coven from the equation, leaving the Daemon and me the time and space we needed to close the portal. I stopped and pulled my hand away, causing her to pause, too. "Let's slow down and take it in. Avrial has not experienced the physical world in this way before."

I'd pulled the name Avrial out of my ass, but this only seemed to fascinate Sister Y. "Your Daemon shared his name with you. Praise Satan!" She clasped her hands together in front of her chest like a giddy schoolgirl.

"I don't know how I knew that…"

"It's okay. We can walk down slowly. I've never been with someone at the exact moment they went through the metamorphosis before! It's so exciting." There was a bounce in her step that hadn't been there on the way up.

"So tell me," I said carefully, not wanting to overplay my hand. "How long before we can execute the Dark Lord's plans?"

"I see someone is eager to put the scourge of humanity out of its misery," she chirped.

Unbidden, my left eyebrow shot up. "With fifty bombs? Surely we need more than that to eradicate the vermin fully."

She laughed. "We're not going to blow them up, silly. That was the plan initially, but unless we could get hold of a nuke, that would be impossible. We're going to use the bombs to tear open the veil to the Daemonic plane so the legions of Satan can come forth and claim what is rightfully theirs!"

Death's cold grip sliced through me. The terror was so great that I stopped, frozen in shock and horror. Lucifuge slipped into my body and took control, softening my features before Sister Y knew something was amiss. He fashioned a ragged smile on my lips. "That is, indeed a much better plan. Of course, we lose our bodies at that point, such an odd sensation, but easy come, easy go."

Sister Y cackled like an insane harpy. "The physical flesh is a prison."

"I was not informed of the exact time we're doing this, though I assume during Black Rite?" My voice sounded hollow, cold, almost too cold. In my mind, I urged the Daemon to rein it in a bit. None of the others behaved like emotionless automatons and if he was too rigid – it would give us away.

"Yep," Sister Y said, cheerfully bounding ahead of me on the trail.

Fuck, I screamed inwardly. *You're a Daemon, shouldn't you have known this?*

I suspected, but I wasn't sure, Lucifuge said as if it was no big deal. *Let's get back down there, tell Drakaris you're now one of them, then ask to be left alone for some meditation time where we'll work on closing the portal.*

You seem to forget that I'm in danger of losing my life here. They're all going to commit suicide by bomb to crack this portal wide open! In my head, my words, thunderous, reverberated through my skull. Outside, everything was still and quiet except for me and Sister Y's footfalls. Buried in my own mind, I realized I'd basically signed up for a suicide mission. The only way I was getting out of this one alive was if the FBI came in and shut it down, or a bomb went off.

Lucifuge did nothing to address my fears. Instead, he stayed in control of my body the entire way back down to the house, and all through breakfast where the coven members took turn hugging and congratulating me on undergoing *the metamorphosis.* I didn't mind, though. I was much happier stuck in the dark recesses of my own mind, contemplating my mortality and feeling sorry for myself.

CHAPTER 13

Somewhere in there, I had fallen into a sleep-like state, leaving Lucifuge in full control of everything. That was probably my first mistake. I was thrust back into my body while walking from the house, wearing a black robe with the hood down. Around me, the rest of the coven was dressed the same, though their hoods were up. I figured there was a reason my hood was down, so made no move to pull it up. Around my neck, I wore a silver amulet with a single bolt of lightning etched on it. I kept walking.

You fell asleep again, Lucifuge said. *I ate lunch and had to take you to the facilities to evacuate your bladder. That was quite the experience.*

I almost laughed out loud at that but turned my mind to more serious matters. *What are we doing?*

Black Rite, Lucifuge said.

Why didn't you wake me up? I tripped on a rock, stumbled but luckily regained my footing. "Sorry," I mumbled to the hooded figures around me.

This portal is taxing on your body and your spirit. You needed the rest. I need you at full strength, he said.

The procession stopped behind the garage at a circular concrete slab with an altar made of granite. Drakaris stepped up next to the altar and motioned the rest of us to gather around.

It was already night.

It's only three in the afternoon, Lucifuge said.

Whereas the world beyond the portal was bright and sunny, the world inside its radius had grown gray and dark. It was like being trapped in a box with hundreds of other creatures, fighting for air and space. To be honest, I was getting a bit tired of portals. First, the portal at Kylie Ramone's mansion, and now this. Gateways to the realm of the dead were just as bad as entrances to an astral plane where darkness and decay loomed. The putrefaction quality of this particular gateway made my skin crawl. Being among the writhing entities was like walking through a pool of stirring earthworms. My skin bristled against their cold, damp astral forms. Lucifuge's energy remained solid against the back of my neck, allegedly feeding off of my corporeal life force.

I turned my attention to what Drakaris was saying. Now donned in black ceremonial robes with the hood up, he wore a purple stole around his neck, embroidered with inverse crosses at both ends. The stole draped over his shoulders and rested against his thick chest. "It is time for Satan to judge the worthiness of our Sister S!"

Sinestria, I thought with an inner snort. He might as well have called me Dark Mistress Sinestria 666. I pressed my eyes closed and inhaled the murk deeply, choking on pestilence. I wondered if I was holding my breath, or if the portal was slowly cutting off my oxygen.

"Step forward, Sister, and receive the Dark Lord's judgment." He motioned me to the front of the crowd, and up to the front of the altar. My heart skipped a beat when I saw the large hunting knife, gleaming in the candlelight. Flame reflected off the edge of the blade, making the sharp steel all the more menacing. One side was serrated, just in case they really had to dig into flesh and bone. I gulped.

You're tense, Lucifuge said. *Everything will be fine.*

But there was something on the edge of the Daemon's voice that gave me pause. I almost balked, but by Lucifuge's divine hand, my feet kept moving forward until I stood facing the crowd of robed acolytes.

Drakaris placed his right hand on my chest, and every inch of me froze, anticipating death. The high priest cleared his throat, closed his eyes, and began speaking in tongues. Pure gibberish.

Not gibberish, Lucifuge said matter-of-factly. *The language of these spirits.*

What's he saying? I asked.

He's telling the other spirits to communicate with the spirit attached to you to make sure you have been properly converted, and saying that if you are not, they will open your chest and feast on your flesh and life force - your blood.

I felt faint but drew in a breath to keep from falling. *Great, I'd rather be blown up by homemade bombs,* I thought. My insides quivered at the thought of being carved up like a turkey dinner on an altar in the middle of the mountains. The air around me moved, and two of the bigger guys standing at either side of the altar approached me, taking me by the arms, pulling me back toward the altar until my back was horizontal with the cold slab of stone. Initially, I began to panic, and my natural reaction was to pull away, but then Lucifuge's calming essence ran through my every pore, and I submitted to my fate.

Sethial picked up the knife. I closed my eyes.

Oh, ye of little faith, Lucifuge said. In that brief moment, I saw a vision of the Daemon in my mind's eye. Humanoid in shape, horned like the mythology, and with intense gold eyes. Those eyes. You could always tell a Daemon by its eyes. The Daemon's mouth moved, growing into a pleasant smile. Around me, I heard whisperings of the strange language, many voices - too many. Then Lucifuge's voice pierced them. *I promised I would not let harm come to you. Now let's finish what we started. Close the portal.*

Now!? Obediently I shoved through the din, finding my astral temple and feeling my body fall free as I rose from it. The temple loomed before me, and I dove for it, slicing into it and closing the aperture behind me. Now, standing on the marble floors in the great temple, I looked around, comforted by the tall stone statues of Astaroth and Belial that stood sentry. I looked toward the altar to find Lucifuge standing there, just a shadow but with those same eyes.

"We have little time. Quickly!" His voice was as clear as if we were both in a physical place and he was standing before me. He motioned me toward him and the altar. The black marble altar, which had been empty before, now held all the tools I would need to close the portal.

The steps of the rite raced through my anxious brain. The ritual worked in three parts. First - I had to banish everything back into the portal by fumigating the area with the banishing incense. Second, I would need to close the portal by drawing its edges together and sealing it with an energy fusing. Finally, I had to perform a second fumigation to make sure nothing was left behind.

The incense, already compiled, sat on the altar. My mind catalogued the ingredients even as I took them up: equal parts of white sandalwood, frankincense, and sage, all thoroughly mixed and heaped in a bowl next to an already hot charcoal in the brass thurible. I didn't bother to be dainty or careful. Instead, I grabbed a tablespoon of the incense with my fingers and dropped it onto the charcoal. The incense sprung to life and began smoldering, sending plumes of thick, fragrant smoke rising into the air. I picked up the thurible and swung it clockwise, willing the temple's cathedral ceiling to open, revealing the open portal. The incense rose skyward, the excessive smoke, more than what the incense would have produced in the physical world, wafted into the darkness. That's when I heard them - screaming. Thousands of creatures writhing in agony.

The words came to me, and I shouted them as loud as I could: "In the Name of Satan, in the name of the Daemonic Divine, I banish all back from whence it came! You are not welcome here! Leave us in peace!" My voice echoed like thunder, lifting upward and out into the entire portal rift.

Then I heard the vibration of the intonation of a Daemonic enn from behind me. I had no idea what Lucifuge was saying or who or what he was invoking, but whatever it was, it seemed to lend strength to my own words. The incense continued to bellow upward, thickened so much that when I looked up, I could see nothing but clouds of gray, hazy smoke. The creatures still screamed and, from the sound of it, they were retreating.

A loud crack sounded from above, and I stopped.

"Keep going," Lucifuge shouted. "They can't get in here; it's heavily warded, though they will try!"

I made it back to the altar to refresh my incense, again traversing the room, swinging the thurible clockwise and shouting the exorcism so that I felt emotion and intent in every syllable.

CRACK! I looked up, half expecting to see the creatures manifest from the smoke and drop down into the ritual space for a hand-to-hand battle. But I kept moving, kept yelling the words, kept fighting.

"Now fuse it!" Lucifuge's voice sent my every pore into flight mode. His entire vibration had changed and standing in his presence became more difficult, but I focused.

I could feel the portal all around us even though I could not see it through the layer of smoke. I raised my hands above my head and drew in a deep breath. Reaching into my heart chakra, the core of my being, I found my inner light and thrust it outward until my entire body emanated blinding brilliance. Then I shoved the light outward, imagining the portal tiny compared to my energy, encompassing it like a blanket, smothering it. I drew the portal, edge to edge, closer and closer until it was pulled together and no more than a slit. Then I intoned Lucifuge's enn. "Eyen tasa valocur Lucifuge Rofocale! Eyen tasa valocur Lucifuge Rofocale. Eyen tasa valocur Lucifuge Rofocale."

I could feel the Daemon's essence emboldening my own, and then with laser focus, I began to fuse the portal shut. The noise from the other side dissipated, becoming more distant with every inch of the portal I fused together until it was dead silent. Finally, I envisioned a violet light filled with strength and warding, and placed it across the scarred veil - solidifying it with a single word, "Resist."

With that final task complete, I dropped to my knees, falling forward. Then, I was on my back, looking up at Lucifuge. I could see him clearly now, more clearly than I had ever seen a Daemon. His caramel skin was flawless, and his golden eyes warm. He reached his hand down, a perfectly manicured strong hand, and lifted me from the ground.

Then I felt warmth on my face.

Just as quickly as I had been pulled onto the altar, I felt the hands holding me down release. Then Drakaris' voice echoed through the void into the real world, "Sister S is found worthy!"

At that moment, the entire abyss sighed with relief, as did I. I opened my eyes, immediately blinded by the bright sunlight staring back at me and shimmied myself off of the altar and back onto my feet.

The entire coven was there, still dressed in their ritual robes, in the bright of day. Excited whispers flew through those assembled. They seemed to be confused by what had just happened. Drakaris tried to play it off as if it was perfectly normal.

Look at their necks, Lucifuge whispered.

I looked at Drakaris, and one by one, I scanned the hooded acolytes. The feeders were gone. Better yet, I could breathe, and I drew the fresh mountain air deep into my lungs. It was light and crisp again. I wondered then if they still wanted to blow themselves up. I didn't have to wait long for the answer.

Drakaris, wild-eyed, as if he had just remembered everything that happened, glanced at the explosive nearest to him. A rush of horrified shouts ran through the coven. That's when the screaming and running began. I looked to my left, my nearest escape. I ran toward the road, all the while yelling into the sweatshirt, "The bombs are going to go off!"

I don't remember how far I got. I just heard the loud, reverberating explosion and felt my body being thrown forward. Then everything went black.

CHAPTER 14

I came to with my face planted in the dirt and rolled onto my back, staring up at the clear sky. The portal was gone and the air, smelling of smoke, slipped easily into my lungs without that heavy, soggy feeling it had possessed before. Turning my head to the right, I saw what remained of the barn and the gathering spot. Between me and the ritual area, a few bodies lay prone and still. The house was to my left, seemingly untouched by the blast save for a few broken windows, probably shattered from flying debris. Once I gauged where I was, in the grassy, weedy area about five feet from the driveway, I moved my attention to my limbs. Dull muscular pain ran the length of my spine, but I could feel my legs, feet, arms, and hands. I drew my right hand up and looked at it. It seemed fine. Then my left, also fine. I lay there a few more minutes listening. I heard tires crunch over gravel, the sound of vehicles moving closer. Finally, the FBI decided to intervene. *Took them long enough*, I thought.

I could only imagine what was going through Mike's head. At that moment, I resolved that I would not allow myself to be dragged into any more dangerous missions. "You hear that, Lucifuge?" I mumbled under my breath.

Well, we had to close that portal, didn't we? he said.

"Yeah. Climb into my body right now and see how I feel." I pushed myself into a sitting position.

I'm here, just not in control. That was an interesting experience. Then the Daemon sighed. Actually sighed.

Behind me, the FBI SUVs and pickups came to a halt and men started getting out. I looked down at what I was wearing. Black robes and that silver lightening amulet. I didn't see anything that looked like blood. There were no rips in the heavy fabric of the robe.

A fit young man with a cleanly shaven head, stocky but tall, jogged toward me. The vest he wore with bright white letters over his left breast marked him as FBI. It wasn't until he knelt beside me that I pegged him in his early thirties. "Don't move, Ma'am. We have a paramedic coming."

I let out a sigh. "Great. Thank you. I'm Elizabeth Tanner, could you please send Detective Katz or Agent Stan over here?"

The man gave me a brisk nod and stood. "Agent Mitchell!" Then he motioned toward us.

Meanwhile, the area in front of me had filled with at least fifteen men, guns drawn just in case, pausing to check for life signs in the bodies they passed as they moved down toward the clearing by the barn. Since they were standing and moving on, I knew that chances were the people they passed up were gone. The entire forest wasn't on fire, but what was left of the barn was, and if they didn't get that under control, we'd have to get out of there - fast.

"Did anyone call the fire department?" I asked my newfound friend, who seemed to refuse to leave my side to join the others in their search for survivors.

"Yes, Ma'am. We called them the second we heard the blast. They should be here any time." The second he finished his sentence, we both heard the distant sirens. "That would be them."

With a nod, I shifted my weight. I probably could have gotten up, but I was afraid that something was broken or pierced, and I didn't want to find out by moving the wrong way.

"Looks like you were the lucky one," he said, shaking his head. "What the hell happened?"

"Yeah," I agreed, but I didn't answer his question. My empathy kicked in, and I felt a strange sense of loss and sadness. Even for Kara, despite the fact that she annoyed me, and I'd spent the bulk of my time with the coven avoiding her. Sure, I found the coven ridiculous, terrifying even, but I had hoped this would end differently. Maybe with Drakaris and Sethial, and the rest in handcuffs - but not dead. I followed the agent's gaze down the hill. Was it really possible I was the only survivor? And how had I gotten so far away so quickly?

I'd like to think I had a hand in that, but I can't take the credit. I think it had to do with all that running you do, Lucifuge said wryly. *I just shielded you from the flying debris and shrapnel, which I think I did a pretty good job at. Not a scratch.*

Thanks, I thought with more sarcasm than I intended.

I felt him beside me even before I turned my head. When I turned toward him, I was staring straight into Mike's blue eyes. They brimmed with relief. He threw his arms around me, pulling me to him, sending a sharp pain through my lower back. "Oww," I said, my voice muffled against his jacket.

"Did I hurt you? Where are you hurt?" He didn't wait for an answer and immediately set about checking me for damage.

"I'm sore. I sprinted up that hill like a jackrabbit with its ass on fire," I said.

"Thank gods you're in good shape," he said without any acknowledgment of my attempt to lighten the mood, his voice distant while he continued checking me over for injury. When he found nothing, he wrapped a strong arm under my arm and around me. "Can you get up? We'll get you into one of the vehicles, have you checked out by the paramedics when they get here."

I nodded, cringing in preparation for pain as he lifted me to my feet. The pain never came, and other than the muscle aches from having made a record sprint and being thrown to the ground from the blast, I felt fine.

My FBI escort moved to the road to direct the fire trucks and the ambulances where to park, and Mike helped me to the other side of the road where we waited for the paramedics to get situated.

While I was fine physically, I felt like I was collapsing mentally. My brain began the arduous task of processing the entire incident.

It turned out that under the robe I was fully clothed, and once the bulk of black fabric was removed, along with the strange amulet, it further reassured Mike that I was unharmed. The paramedics wrapped a blanket around my shoulders, just in case I was in shock, while Mike insisted that I didn't need to go to the hospital and that I'd follow up with my regular physician the next day. Everything from that point forward was a blur.

Despite the fact that Lucifuge and I had just averted a disaster that could have ended planet earth, a pretty big deal from where I sat, Agent Stan insisted Mike and I head back home. He assured Mike that he'd debrief us later. I was positive it was Stan's way of saying that the FBI's didn't need our help to count bodies and put out fires. He was right.

One of the agents broke away to drive Mike and I back down the mountain and into the city, to the safety and comfort of our house in the foothills. By the time we arrived in the driveway, I felt like I hadn't changed anything. There was no one I could have saved. There was nothing I could have done to change the outcome. The entities attached to the coven members had convinced them that killing themselves in order to further open the portal was the will of Satan himself.

But Lucifuge and I, we'd closed the portal. Me with sheer will and magick, and Lucifuge by providing me the training and strength to do it.

That portal would have endangered life as you know it, Lucifuge reminded me. *The twilight of man is once again pushed into the future.*

Something like this has happened before? I asked, shocked.

As it will happen again, Lucifuge said, a tinge of sadness to his tone.

The human race saved for another day.

I spent the remainder of the day on the couch, grateful for Mike's pampering. I'd told him everything that happened as I remembered it, and he was patient and listened, only asking the occasional question.

"So, wait, the plan wasn't to blow up large venues at all then? But all of our intel..." Mike bit his lower lip and furrowed his brow.

"That may have been the initial plan, but the entities changed that. The *Dark Diocese,* or *Anti-Christs Temple,* was a suicide cult. They were all being controlled by those astral entities. The entities needed a bigger gateway, and to make that happen, apparently, they needed a big explosion at the center of the open portal. All those poor people believed it because the entities were controlling their minds. I think at the last minute, after Lucifuge and I closed the rift, and they had that moment of clarity where they weren't being controlled. They realized too late that they wanted to live and that the bombs were about to go off. I don't think any of them, except Drakaris and Sethial, were guilty. They were just naive and being controlled. Innocent bystanders. Even Kara." I shrugged as I thought about my walk that morning with Sister Y. She had been the only person I'd had a genuine conversation with while I was there aside from Drakaris and Sethial. I felt a tinge of sadness for her.

Mike just nodded and said nothing. He hadn't scolded me yet, but it was the elephant in the room between us.

"Even though we saved the world from a rift full of entities that feed on physical life, I'm never doing anything like that *ever* again," I said decisively, taking a sip from the steaming cup of Black Pekoe he brought me.

He sat down heavily on the couch next to me. "It would probably be best for my blood pressure if you didn't."

I laughed and set the tea on the end table. "Should we make a pact?"

"With blood and everything?" A slow smile spread over his lips.

"If you want." I drew the blanket from the back of the couch and pulled it over my lap.

His cell phone rang. "Hold that thought," he said, getting up to answer.

He spent a good ten minutes in the kitchen, chatting, while I flipped through the streaming channels unable to find anything to watch. I finally settled on a rerun of MASH, a comforting go-to when you didn't feel like thinking or really paying attention, but you wanted the background noise.

Mike finally returned, his expression perplexed.

I muted the television.

"Well, they found the remains of most of the coven members that they knew were there, including Drakaris, but they didn't find Sethial, Yvonne, or your buddy Kara. They think they may have escaped." Mike sat down again. "They searched a three-mile radius, and they're checking the local hospitals. Either they missed them or…."

A sigh of relief erupted from me. The hope that even a few of them escaped death, especially Yvonne who I was sure was Sister Y, warmed me. Three of them escaped. They were the

FBI's problem now. Having FBI agents breathing down their necks was better than having those feeders attached to them. Even if they had to face justice – this way, they had a chance to be free.

That night I called my mother-in-law to check up on wedding plans, and Alyssa to see if she had told Gabe about the baby yet. Beverly had everything under control, of course. Alyssa had told Gabe she was pregnant and, apparently, he was over the moon. There was still no talk of a wedding for those two, and my guess was they likely wouldn't bother. I didn't mention the past few days events to Beverly or Alyssa, and neither of them asked. To them, it had been just a couple of days living their life, a blip in the grander scheme of things. For me, it had felt like weeks. I had almost lost my life - again. It was time for me to hang up my investigative hat and focus on the wedding, my friends, my job, and me and Mike's life together. As I got ready for bed that night, I was happy. Happier than I'd felt in weeks.

Lucifuge?

The Daemon didn't answer my mental call right away.

"Lucifuge? You in there? Hello…" I finally said aloud, looking at my own wary reflection in the bathroom mirror.

I'm here, he finally said.

"Thank you again for saving my ass," I said at my reflection.

You saved your own ass. I just helped you find the strength to do it. Just like your will closed the portal. I was simply there for moral support, he said with practiced pragmatism.

"Well, you did protect me from the shrapnel and debris from the blast," I countered.

Only a little help. You don't need as much help as you seem to think you need, Elizabeth. You have a great well of strength within you.

Willpower of steel. You can do anything you put your mind to, as long as you believe it. I imagined the Daemon smiling as he said that.

"Well, thank you. Knowing you were always there helped." I smiled at myself.

This is it. I will leave you be now, Lucifuge assured me.

Melancholy washed over me, and I let out a forlorn sigh. *I think I might actually miss you.*

Never fear, child of the Daemonic. I am always watching. We shall meet again. I can promise you that. Then, with a mental nod, Lucifuge's presence simply vanished and was no more. No fanfare, no bright lights, no ring of fire on the floor. A half grin slid onto my lips at the realization of how anticlimactic it all was. One minute the Daemon was there and the next, he was gone.

Mike gently knocked on the bathroom door before poking his head in. "You okay?"

I nodded, noticing his eyes were checking my arms, legs, and torso, but not in the way he usually did. He was looking for signs of bruising or missed cuts. "I'm fine," I assured him. Then, as if it was an afterthought, I added, "Lucifuge is gone."

"Thank the gods for that. I can respect a Daemon for needing a host to save the world, but did you tell him to pick someone else next time?" Mike came up behind me, wrapping his arms around me, and looking at my face in the mirror.

"He knows, trust me. We had that discussion." I leaned into him. "So, life goes on tomorrow like none of this ever happened…"

"We know it happened, but yes, life goes on. Hopefully a long, uneventful, rather boring life," he said, his eyes full of hope.

"Agreed," I said.

He kissed my temple. "Well, let's get some sleep. We don't have any wedding stuff to do, do we?"

"Nope. Beverly has it all handled. But I can think of something we can do." I kissed him back, my mouth lingering on his. Just like that, we were focused on our wedding again, and life as we knew it, free from unexpected Daemonic interference, went back to being normal, boring, and happy. For that, I was grateful.

CHAPTER 15

My mother, who'd lost about twenty pounds through a new exercise regimen since my last visit, leaned into me. "Did you know one of Michael's uncles is a warlock?"

I choked up my champagne, craning forward so it would hit the ground instead of my dress. I felt my eyes widen. "Where did you hear that?"

"I asked him about the medallion he's wearing, and he said it's a 'sigil of Hekate'," she said, matter of fact. "Then he went on to tell me that it was consecrated during a ritual of great power."

The food and cake I'd just eaten threatened to come up, but I swallowed. Hard. That helped to keep it all down, including the knot of anxiety now in my chest. "Well, that's eccentric," I said, playing it off.

My mother shook her head. "His side of the family does seem to be on the *interesting* end of things. Which is surprising since he's so down to earth and well-adjusted."

I nodded, searching the sea of family and friends for Mike. I spotted him with Gabe at a table near the gazebo where the cake and the slowly melting ice swans were set up. "I have to go talk to Mike."

"Go ahead, dear. I'm going to go find Beverly." Her eyes searched the stately lawn.

"Don't ask her about her brother's Hekate medallion," I said quickly.

My mother gave me a confused look. "Why would I do that?"

I shrugged and set my now empty champagne flute down on the table next to me, noticing Alyssa, her stomach protruding ever so slightly in the cobalt blue dress, sitting down with Gabe and Mike. "I'll be back," I told my mom before sprinting my way through the crowd, hoping I wouldn't be stopped along the way. The wedding, due to Beverly's meticulous planning and Kenny DeBeer's diligence, had gone without a hitch. I couldn't wait to get away and recover from all the socializing. If I heard what a beautiful bride I was one more time, I was going to scream.

I made it to the table with a forced smile, and by the time I sat in the chair across from Mike, my cheeks burned. "How long before we can get the hell out of here?"

Mike laughed.

Gabe put his arm around Alyssa. "You're the bride, don't you get to decide?"

Alyssa laughed. She reached into a bowl of pistachios on the table and popped one into her mouth.

I reached my arm across the table, taking Mike's hand into mine. "Your uncle Jacob told my mom all about his powerful Hekate amulet."

He laughed again and shook his head. "Oh gods."

"Uh huh. To my mom, it's just scandalous gossip, thank goodness. I think I'm starting to get a headache." I pulled my hand back and rubbed my temples, careful to mind the garland of lavender I wore on my head. Beverly had insisted on it because, as she said, it would relax me. Well, it wasn't working.

"All things considered, it went really well. I don't think anyone in your family realized the High Priest is a witch," Mike said with a half grin.

I had insisted on a more secular ceremony for that reason, much to Beverly's chagrin, but she had been accommodating after I told her I wasn't really *out* with my family. I looked down at my white gown, double checking to make sure I hadn't stained it already. What I really wanted was to get out of the uncomfortable dress, climb into a hot bath, and relax in silence for a few hours.

There was a clanking of metal on glass, and the crowd mulling the lawn stopped and went silent, their attention shifting to Mike's uncle Jacob who stood on the stage where the band had been playing only a half hour ago. He wore a rumpled suit with the top three buttons undone on his white shirt, and he looked like he hadn't shaved in a few days. "Thank you for your attention," he said in a deep baritone. The Hekate amulet around his neck glinted in the late afternoon sunlight. "My coven has a special gift for the bride and groom."

My heart stopped in my chest.

Mike let out a nervous laugh, a hint of crimson flushing his cheeks. "Shit, here we go."

Drumming erupted all around us, and we whirled around in our chairs to find the entire reception area surrounded by drummers adorned in full ritual robes. They made their way to the front of the stage, and once they were lined up - the drumming stopped.

"For the blood-born warlock, my nephew Michael, the groom, and his charming soulmate and bride Elizabeth, the Daemonolatress, beloved of Lucifuge. May Hekate bless your union always," Jacob bellowed into the microphone.

What happened next will be seared in my memory, and the memory of my family, for decades to come. A naked woman, holding aloft a cobalt blue satin pillow, emerged from the crowd toward us. On the pillow was a wand.

Mike and I glanced at one another in horror for a brief moment, then back at the woman - who stopped before the table.

My eyes searched the crowd quickly for a way out, but all I saw were the smiles on the faces of Mike's family, smiles on the faces of my co-workers and witchy friends, and utter shock on the faces of the members of my family.

Was I just mentioned? It was Lucifuge.

Oh shit, not now, I thought, my heart sinking. I began to feel faint.

No, you don't, he said giving me a quick jolt of energy. The Daemon jumped into my body, but he didn't shove me aside. Instead, he merged with me and together we looked around.

I see the appeal in this ritual, he said. *Congratulations to you and Mike on a successful pair-bonding.*

Then, with my hand, Lucifuge reached out and took up the wand from the pillow.

"For fertility and magick, and a happy life!" Jacob finished. He lifted his glass. "Let's drink to Michael and Elizabeth!"

The crowd, including my very confused family, lifted their glasses and everyone drank.

I'm sorry I missed the cake, but I just wanted to say goodbye since we won't be working so closely now, Lucifuge said in my mind's eye. *However, if you ever need me, I am here for you.*

Thanks, Lucifuge. You'll always be one of my favorite Daemons, I thought back. Then I handed the wand to Mike with another cheek burning smile.

The vibrating sensation of Lucifuge's presence dissipated quickly, leaving me heart racing and a bead of sweat on my brow.

Mike, with the wand in hand, nodded toward his uncle. "Thank you, uncle Jacob. And thanks to all of you for coming today. We are truly blessed to have such wonderful friends and family, and your presence has made this celebration memorable."

There was applause and laughter and the crowd drifted back to mingling. I sat heavily back in the chair. "I really need to get out of this dress," I said, taking Alyssa's watch strapped wrist into my hand to check the time. It had been almost three hours since the reception started.

"Well," Beverly said from behind me, causing me to jump. My mother trailed her, none worse for the wear after I'd been outed as a word she probably didn't understand and after seeing a naked woman parade through my wedding. She grabbed another champagne from a passing tray and rushed to keep up with Beverly, who said quickly, "Shouldn't you two be off and getting ready for your honeymoon?"

Mike looked at his watch. "Our plane for Hawaii does leave in five hours, and I'm pretty sure Liz could use some rest."

I nodded, extremely thankful.

Beverly gave me a knowing look. We stood and said our goodbyes, Mike with the wand in hand. As weddings went - I was glad it was over.

As we made our way toward the house, Mike tapped the wand against his hand.

"Fertility wand, you think?" I asked.

"Probably something like that. I have no idea if we're supposed to display it, or what." He turned it over in his hands as we strode away from the reception.

"You do realize we're going to have to keep our families separated as much as possible, right," I said, glancing over my shoulder. "I don't know how many more naked, gift-bearing women my mother will be able to handle."

Mike let out a hearty chuckle. "I'm not going to live that down with the guys at work, either."

I hadn't even considered that. "We're going to have a lot of explaining to do to those not in-the-know when we get back from Hawaii."

"Yep," Mike said. "But let's forget about it for now, Mrs. Katz."

"Oh, by the way," I said, lifting my dress a little so I could walk faster. "Lucifuge stopped by to congratulate us and say goodbye."

Mike shot me a surprised look and he smiled. "Well, I'm glad to hear that."

I took his hand into mine. "Let's go enjoy some sun-kissed beaches and lava fields."

We both laughed and slipped around the side of the house to the car. All the while I knew our lives would never be the same. The past was the past. Today was the start of something new.

THIRTEEN COVENS: DARKNESS

A full week in Hawaii had done Mike and I a lot of good. We were relaxed and still had a couple of weeks before we had to get back to work. When the phone rang, even though I didn't recognize the number and I knew it was a bad idea, I picked up anyway.

"Liz - hey, it's Darren Steele, Rhode Island."

"Darren?" This seemed more than coincidence. I'd just been thinking about the investment banker not long ago as I was going over me and Mike's investment portfolios, as pathetic as they were. Darren was a huge supporter of the Ordo Templi Serpentis, the order where I formerly volunteered as a public relations officer, and the Black Magick Network, where I now worked as the Program Director. He regularly gave donations to the Black Magick Network's charitable organization. The charity gave college scholarships to young practicing magicians whose winning essays on magick were published annually in the *Black Magick Journal*. Darren Steele had been interviewed on Magistra Collette's *Magick Today* show more than once, though I'd only met him the last time he was on.

"The one and only. Hey, I called to ask you a question. You got a moment?" His voice sounded deeper than I remembered it.

Wary about why a man I barely knew would be calling me at home, I said, "Sure, shoot."

"I know it's short notice, but how would you and Mike like to come take a mini-vacation with me and my wife, Ellen?"

My sense of impending doom grew. How he'd gotten my home number was a mystery in itself. I decided to ask more questions. "Well, I suppose that depends. We just got back from our honeymoon in Hawaii."

"Oh, I heard. Congratulations on finally tying the knot." He didn't acknowledge my qualifier. "Have you heard of Haileyville, New York?"

Everyone had heard of Haileyville. "The town where practically everyone is a magician? Who hasn't? The BMN gets a lot of orders out of there."

"Uh huh. My family lives up there, as you probably know, I have some ties to a few of the covens. One of my good friends owns a bed and breakfast just outside of town. Said I could have a couple of rooms over Beltane if I booked by this weekend. I immediately thought of you and your husband. You guys game?" He sounded hopeful.

"I didn't know you had family up there..." I racked my brain, trying to remember if he'd ever told me about it. Oh, people claimed to have friends or family in the Thirteen all the time, but most of them were liars. Darren, on the other hand - something about the tone of his voice told me I should believe him.

"It's not something I really advertise because, you know, people try to get in good with you just so you'll introduce them," he said. "The covens don't like outsiders."

So why was he asking me? I furrowed my brow. A lot of people took pilgrimages up to the tri-county area of upstate

New York hoping to catch a public ritual or glimpse something magical. They usually came back with tales of Daemonic churches and public liturgical rites and said things like, "Everyone was so nice!" I'd always wanted to go myself, but the opportunity had never presented itself. Plus, it seemed kind of creepy to go to a town of witches and Daemonolaters just to gawk at them. They were people for Daemon's sake. Not zoo animals.

However, if I were a cat, I'd likely be dead because my curiosity, like usual, got the better of me. "Okay, I'll bite. You could have asked anyone, but you chose me - practically a stranger…"

There was a pause. Here it came. "We need your help with something, and just figured since you were one of us, and you've worked with law enforcement before…"

"I'm retired from that kind of work," I said quickly. My heart started thumping in my chest. "It was getting a bit too dangerous for me and Mike's liking."

"I'm pretty sure this isn't dangerous." His words didn't match his tone.

"On a scale of one to ten?" My eyes narrowed.

His hesitance was painfully apparent now. "I can't really give you details on the phone, but suffice to say we need someone impartial, who isn't part of *The Thirteen* to work with the council on a matter."

"You need a mediator?" I could scarcely believe my ears.

"Kind of. The covens have been getting out of line a bit and that usually falls to Blackrose, but no one trusts that they're impartial, and they want an unbiased investigator to help Sheriff Steve get to the bottom of some shenanigans. We can't really bring in an outsider for this. I'm sure you understand," he explained, his voice rising in pitch a little.

My heart beat a little faster. "If you can promise that I won't be shot at, kidnapped, molested, or harmed in any way, I would think about it."

"Nothing like that. No murders or anything. This is… well, I can't really explain it now. It's a keep silent type of thing. I'm sure you understand." He was beginning to sound unsure again.

I let out a sigh. "Alright. Go ahead and count us in. I still have to ask Mike, but I'm sure I can sway him. I've always wanted to see what it would be like to live in a town with all witches, pagans, and Daemonolaters. Of course, you realize my boss will try to talk me into bringing a camera crew, right?"

A forced laugh emerged from him. "Well then, this is the perfect opportunity to meet people and see if they'd let a camera crew in at a later date. If it's a working research trip, you get paid for it, right?"

I couldn't deny his logic. "Right…" All the while, the fact that he couldn't tell me much nagged at me. After all, why would the covens talk to me? I may have been one of them in practice, but I was still an outsider. "But Darren, what makes you think anyone will open up to me?"

There was a pause, then he said, "Your reputation precedes you. Plus, you write books that Eve Winters can't keep on Black Raven's shelves. I have a feeling you might get further than Sheriff Steve. If you come, we can talk about it when you arrive, and if you turn us down, then no harm, no foul. You get a nice vacation out of it."

"The council wants me?" I asked, hoping I could prod him for more information.

Darren ignored the question. "I'll have my secretary set up the flight and get back with you on details."

"Okay," I said uncertainly. If the trip was paid for, Mike would have to say yes.

"Good. I look forward to seeing you again," he said, his voice triumphant. "Email me if you have questions or things change. You do have my email, right?"

"I do."

His voice went cheery again. "Good, talk soon!"

After I'd hung up, I stared in disbelief at the phone. I'd probably just opened the door to another ration of shit and broken my promise to Mike in the process. After all, where there were magicians there were at least a few legit magicians, and where there were legit magicians, there was always trouble. Haileyville, New York was packed to the brim with legit magicians.

I thought it through, mulling over how the Thirteen Covens knew all about my work on the cases of Chloe Brigid, Kylie Ramone, and Lucien Groner. That made sense, of course, since Darren Steele was a big fan of the Black Magick Network. So, while the covens did keep to themselves, the council watched. Or someone did. At least a few of them had to know something of what was going on outside their coven-bubble. He hadn't even told me which of the covens he had ties to, but I figured I'd find out soon enough.

Mike strolled into the kitchen and went to the fridge, opening it and peering inside. "Who was that?"

"You know the investment banker from New York? Darren Steele? Big supporter of the Black Magick Network?" I knew he didn't know, but I was trying to play it cool. It had been such a nice day that I didn't want to ruin it by telling him that I'd agreed to something where the details were still a mystery.

"I think you mentioned him. The guy who gave a lot of money to the scholarship thing?" Mike pulled himself from the fridge and shut the door.

"Yeah, he invited us up to Haileyville, New York over Beltane." Then I heard the lie come out of my mouth as if I'd been rehearsing it for weeks. "I think he wants to schmooze and talk business. Probably wants to pitch a show to me. Though he insists he had an extra room at the B&B he was staying at and thought it might be nice to get to know you and me more."

Mike narrowed his eyes. I'd overplayed my hand. "He definitely wants something."

"Yeah, mentioned something about me possibly being able to write it off as a business expense for scouting a... show. Ohhh!" I nodded at Mike knowingly, while inwardly cringing at my outright fabrication.

"Yep." Mike laughed. "Did you say yes?"

"I told him to go ahead and count us in, but it was still up to you." At least I knew I was still capable of telling some truth.

"Do you want to go?" Mike's eyes went to the calendar. "Do we have any plans over Beltane?"

"No plans, but maybe we should go. Maybe he has a good pitch. He is related to one of the Thirteen Covens," I said, carefully. "Plus, he said he was paying."

"Babe, how did you not know this was a schmooze?" He shook his head, a great big grin plastered on his face. "We'll go. It could be fun."

I nodded. "I'll email him and tell him it's a go."

His focus quickly changed. "When's dinner?"

"About an hour," I said.

After he left the room, I collapsed into the bar stool at the end of the kitchen island and put my head in my hands. I'd have to email Darren and tell him to keep what we'd talked about between us for now. When Mike found out the covens wanted me as an impartial judge, or investigator, or whatever it was exactly — he was going to be pissed. If he knew that I knew about it going in - he would be really pissed.

FINIS

Dear Reader - I want to thank you wholeheartedly for sticking with me through the entire OTS series. Does this mean Liz's adventures have come to an end? Not at all. She's going into coven territory for a crossover story next, and I have several outlines for shorter Liz adventures that may manifest sporadically over the next few years. In the meantime, if you enjoyed Liz and Mike's adventures, definitely watch for Thirteen Covens: Darkness, the crossover that will introduce you to my award-winning Thirteen Covens series! I've been asking people if they're ready to choose a side and soon, you'll know why.

I'm also rather excited about my new Djinn & Bourbon urban fantasy series that has been in the brainstorming and preliminary writing stages for a few years now. Have you ever wondered what would happen if a young man inherited a Djinn from his odd uncle, only to discover he's the last Protectorate of the Vessels? Inherited Djinn, Book One of the Djinn and Bourbon series, answers that very question. Meet Bill MacPhegor (the awkward guy), Hemlock Samhaish (the weird girl), and Bill's cigarette smoking, bourbon swilling, foul-mouthed guardian Djinn, Paimon (yeah, *that* Paimon). I can give you 72 reasons you'll be delighted to meet my fictionalized Djinn. Coming soon (provided the publishing schedule works out this year).

Want to be alerted the next time I release something new? Join my newsletter at:

http://www.audreybrice.com/newsletter/

Thank you so much for reading!

Sign up for the Audrey Brice Newsletter to receive **free fiction** and updates on Thirteen Covens, the OTS Series, and other releases!

About the Author

Audrey Brice is the pseudonym of a renowned Daemonolatress and practicing magician who has been performing her artes since the mid-eighties. She lives with her husband and several cats along the front range of the beautiful Rocky Mountains.

Also by Audrey Brice

Outer Darkness

When socialite Chloe Brigid is murdered and the crime seems to have occult overtones, outed daemon worshiper Senator Steve Mitchell is arrested. It's up to magician Elizabeth Tanner, the public figurehead of the Ordo Templi Serpentis, to find out who outed the senator and who killed Chloe Brigid before the senator is falsely accused of the crime and The Order is investigated. What she finds, however, is not what she expects. The killer's attention soon turns toward her. Will she be able to help the police find the killer before she becomes the next victim?

Into Darkness

Magus Elizabeth Tanner has been gifted some cursed magickal items. While trying to break the curse, she and her boyfriend Michael become suspects in a murder they didn't commit. To clear their names they must find the real killer by delving into a dark bdsm underworld where sex magick and the Daemonic meet. Will they be able to find a killer, clear their names, and escape their descent into darkness?

Also Available
Rising Darkness, Ascending Darkness, Dead Man's Knock, When Good Angels Go Bad,
Sunny Satan Arizona, Rocky Mountain Haunt, Within Darkness (paperback of the OTS novellas), Stygian: Disciples Thirteen Covens: A Rising Damp, Temple Apophis, Lucifer's Haven, Shadow Marbas, The Watch, Ba'al Collective, Order of Eurynome, (Bloodlines Part One includes the first 7 stories), Blackrose Coven, Temple Dagon

Forthcoming:
Thirteen Covens: Darkness
Cult of Lucifuge

By Audrey Brice as Anne O'Connell

Training Amy

When Amy starts her new job at a book shop she has no idea what kind of merchandise her two bosses have stored in a private back room for select customers. She's never been allowed back there. One night, when she's closing shop alone she decides to take a look. Big mistake. Brad and Eric (her bosses) catch her snooping around. They don't tolerate rule-breakers and Amy must be punished. Will her secret desires plunge her deeper into their world? Or will she run back to the safety of her normal life and the dull boyfriend who has a dark side of his own?

Publisher's Note: This book contains explicit sexual content, graphic language, and situations that some readers may find objectionable: BDSM theme and content includes: dubious consent, bondage, spanking, toys, anal play, and menage m/f/m and m/f/f.

Other Titles:
Weekend Captive, Sincerely, Megan
Nice Girls Don't, My Neighbor Enslaved
Switched, Domme X, The Rite, DOM359
Her Demon Lover, Her Demon Wedding
Black Lily, Temple of Lilith, Taming Trish

Forthcoming From Anne O'Connell:
Falling from Grace, Her Demon Master

By Audrey Brice as S. J. Reisner

Left Horse Black (Sorcerers' Twilight Book 1)

For centuries, the zealot Kersian sorcerers have abducted innocent women and children for sacrifice to their 'no name' god and have waged war upon Danaria's sorcerers. Now, they are covertly usurping the thrones of human-ruled kingdoms to do the unthinkable; they are building a massive human army to assist them in destroying Danaria's sorcerer bloodlines in an attempt to save their own. Armed with nothing more than meager weapons, untrained sorcery, and mere instinct, a troubled human prince, an inept Danarian sorceress, and their friends, rise up and become the world's last hope to stop the Kersians, and save the sorcerers' dying race. Will they succeed?

Other Titles:

Warrior's Blood Red (Sorcerers' Twilight Book 2)
Saving Sarah May (Contemporary Romance)

Forthcoming:

Eagle's Talon Gray (Sorcerers' Twilight Book 3)

www.ingramcontent.com/pod-product-compliance
Lightning Source LLC
Chambersburg PA
CBHW031235260626
47169CB00007B/2311